Emma Berry Mystery series

Saddled with Death
A Gem of a Problem
A Body in the Woodpile
Murder at the Mill
Death in Disguise

DEATH in DISGUISE

An Emma Berry Mystery
Book #5

Irene Sauman

Jakada Books

PERTH, WESTERN AUSTRALIA

Author's Note

The Emma Berry mysteries are set in the eighteen-seventies on the Murray River, the third longest navigable river in the world, surpassed only by the Amazon and the Nile. Its great navigable length was responsible for the development of the riverboats, the sidewheel paddle steamers that opened up the Australian countryside along the river's length to settlement and sheep farming, in much the way railways did in the wider countryside.

Indeed, it was the railways that eventually ended the glory days of the paddle steamers, though they continue to ply the waters in the twenty-first century, carrying tourists and holidaymakers. Two generations of my father's family produced working riverboat captains. But this story is strictly fiction.

Death in Disguise is the fifth title in the series.

Main Characters

Emma Berry: wife & mother, herbalist

Daniel Berry: Emma's husband, Captain of the PS *Mary B*

Darcy Berry: their 7-year-old son

Janey Wirra: Emma's maid of all work,

Abe Miller: Janey's man, and Emma's man of all work,

Old Mr. Pickles: head of the Pickles family

Henrietta Pickles: his daughter-in-law, Emma's friend, & part-owner of the Primrose Tearoom with...

Janet Naughton (nee Pickles): her daughter

Alex Naughton: Janet's husband, livery stable owner

Nathaniel Pickles: Henrietta's estranged husband, senior clerk at Echuca wharf

Charity Pickles: Nathaniel's sister, manages Pickles boarding house where her father and brother live

Grace Hewitt (nee Pickles): Charity & Nathaniel's sister, a widow, visiting the family

Miriam Hewitt: her daughter,

Jonathan Inglis: Miriam's fiancé, a young barrister

Henry Collins: a businessman

Dr. MacArthur: Coroner

Sergeant Donovan: police officer in charge of Echuca Police Station

Henry Collins: a businessman

Dr. MacArthur: Coroner

Sergeant Donovan: police officer in charge of
Echuca Police Station

Mr. Samuel Rasmussen: of Kentish, Rasmussen and
Foyle, attorneys

Mrs. Gloria Rasmussen: his wife, member of the
Ladies Benevolent Society

Delia Rasmussen: their daughter

Echuca Ladies Benevolent Society - The visitors reported on several parties now receiving funds from the Society. These matters involved considerable discussion and adjustment; eventually it was resolved to increase the allowance given to several of the old pensioners on the funds. *Riverine Herald, Tuesday 4 July 1882, p.3*

Chapter 1
Emma Speaks Out

September 1884

THE MEETING room in the Echuca Town Hall buzzed with conversation as members of the Ladies Benevolent Society gathered for their annual general meeting. Emma Berry and her friend Henrietta Pickles took their seats amidst the chatter and fashionable outfits.

At the back of the room, behind two long tables, three young women in maids' uniform of black dress and white pinafore, were setting out teapots, sugar bowls, cups, plates of cakes and scones, and anything else needed for a smart afternoon tea. A large urn steamed in one corner.

Emma imagined the maids had been supplied by some of the well-heeled ladies present whose husbands were involved in the river or timber trade, perhaps even a riverboat captain. She could have offered Janey's services. Whether her lovely, outspoken Janey would have appreciated it would have been another matter.

A white cloth, with the Society's name embroidered in blue on the front, covered the table on the raised stage at the top of the room, and on either side of the stage a tall vase, containing blue and pink hydrangeas with greenery, added colour.

"I see Henry Collins is here," Henrietta said sotto voce. "No doubt he will pat himself on the back for some clever thing he's done or have some criticism to make about what we're doing."

"Oh, does he not agree with the Society's work?" Emma asked, exchanging a nod with a lady in her street who she knew slightly. She'd only been a fulltime resident in the town for two months and was still finding her way. If it weren't for Henrietta and her daughter, Janet, she would have struggled to find acceptance.

As if marrying her brother-in-law, a year after her husband's death weren't enough, she had travelled on a riverboat with Daniel and their all-male crew for most of that year. She knew propriety had been maintained but it would have been a waste of time trying to explain that to anyone. Her mother had warned her, as had her grandmother.

Henrietta wrinkled her nose and leaned closer. "Oh yes. He's very supportive. But we are only women after all and cannot possibly do anything without a man to guide us." The irony in her words was not lost on Emma. Henrietta was separated from her husband, Nathaniel Pickles, and ran the successful Primrose Tearoom with Janet. She saw no need for a man to manage her life.

Emma understood Henrietta's feelings perfectly. Travelling on a riverboat had brought her into contact with men of all temperaments, not least of all her crew members and their erstwhile captain, now her darling husband.

"Which one is he?" she asked now. There were three men standing at the front of the room, in conversation with two smartly dressed ladies.

"The short, stout one with the bushy moustache. He's talking at our secretary, Mrs. Watson-Smith."

Talking 'at' was an apt description. There was tension in that group. Mrs. Watson-Smith's white-gloved hands were gripping her folder of papers to the point of distorting its shape.

"Oh dear."

"Indeed. The mayor appointed him his representative as patron of the Society, more to get him out of his own hair than anything, I suspect. Though according to Anna Marshall – the mayor's wife, that is – it isn't working out very well. Henry Collins is her cousin you know."

Emma hadn't known. She had a vague recollection of meeting Anna Marshall somewhere, at some time, but she didn't think Henry Collins had been a subject of discussion. She was discovering, however, that she needed to tread carefully in her social interactions for fear of tripping up on relationships she wasn't aware of.

"Is the other lady the president?" she asked.

Henrietta nodded. "Mrs. Augustus. Very efficient. She's been president for six years now."

Eventually, the two Committee ladies and Mr. Collins took their seat at the table, facing the assembled group, while the other two gentlemen found seats in the front row.

Mrs. Augustus welcomed everyone and spoke generally of the good work that had been done during the year in relieving the distress of residents who found themselves in hard times, through no fault of their own. This last remark seemed to bear a slight emphasis and brought a telling 'hmph' from Mr. Collins. Mrs. Augustus looked as if she had a bad smell under her nose as she went on with her speech, detailing who had been helped, why, and how.

One family, she explained, had lost their home in a fire caused by a log rolling out of the grate. Accommodation, clothing, and other essential items had been found for them. Another man was off work for several months due to an accident while cutting wood. He had a large family and had been unable to provide for them during that time.

As Mrs. Augustus spoke, Mr. Collins seemed to find something of great interest on the ceiling. His casual, and almost dismissive, attitude was not accepted in complete silence. A growing restlessness was permeating the audience. There was some rustling, and the occasional clearing of throats, but deference to Mrs. Augustus prevented anything further. When she ended her speech, the audience gave her more than just polite applause, as if in compensation for the man's rudeness, and perhaps to send him a message.

"Something must have annoyed him," Henrietta whispered. "He's behaving very badly, even for him."

Mrs. Watson-Smith rose to read the treasurer's report, in lieu of the treasurer, Mrs. Anna Marshall, who was unable to attend due to a family emergency. Emma wondered if the emergency involved avoiding her cousin.

Her mind wandered as the figures being read out for the incomings and outgoings created a soporific effect. She found herself watching Henry Collins, as his disinterest in proceedings continued and was only brought back to the moment when Mrs. Watson-Smith declared herself supremely happy to report that the Society had ended the year with twenty pounds in its account. This was greeted with another burst of applause. Emma thought with amusement that the applause might also be a result of relief that the treasurer's report, rather long and detailed, had been brought to a close.

As Mrs. Watson-Smith sat, Mr. Collins got to his feet, thrusting his hands into his trouser pockets.

"Thank you, ladies, for those most interesting reports," he said, inclining his head politely to the two ladies beside him. "I must congratulate the Society on its benevolent work over the past twelve months," he went on, stepping out from behind the table and taking centre stage. "I guess we, as a caring society, will always be called on to support those who are unable to take proper care of themselves, and you have excelled yourselves in that."

The ladies at the table seemed to relax and Mrs. Augustus almost allowed herself a smile.

"But I must say," Mr. Collins went on, his voice rising on a note of disbelief, "I was most surprised and disappointed to hear that you hold twenty pounds in reserve. That is a significant amount to have on hand, unused. One has to ask, how diligent have you been in searching out these needy people? Surely there must have been others you could have spent these monies on? All the fuss with fund raising, and requests for donations that you've made over the year, and you haven't even spent it all."

A collective intake of breath from those present seemed to draw the air out of the room. You could have heard the proverbial pin drop for a moment, before bewildered whispers, like a gentle breeze, swept the room. But no one, not even the Society's secretary or president, stood up to refute the criticism.

Emma's eyes narrowed. Before she had time to think she found herself on her feet. "Mr. Collins, your respect for the less fortunate becomes you," she began, her voice carrying a measured strength, and a note of irony that drew a quickly muffled titter from someone. "But it is precisely because of the reserve funds that the Society has been able to provide ongoing support to those in need." There was a hum of agreement, punctuated by approving nods from some of the ladies. Emma's confidence rose.

"We cannot offer financial support in the case of an emergency if we have no money available," she continued. "The reserve is not a mere luxury, but a necessity, a safety net for those whose lives may hang in the balance at any moment. We cannot know what tomorrow may bring but thank heaven we have caring people in our community to lend a hand when unforeseen events occur to upset our lives. We hope the day will never come that we need such assistance ourselves, but we will be eternally grateful that it is there if we ever do. I personally congratulate our committee for their foresight and their excellent financial management."

Emma put her hands together and her applause was quickly taken up around the room, several women rising to their feet as they clapped amid cries of "hear, hear," from several directions.

Mr. Collins appeared taken aback by Emma's response and its acceptance by those present. He glowered in her direction. Henrietta patted Emma's arm as she regained her seat.

"Well done," she whispered, "though I fear you have made an enemy."

Mr. Collins cleared his throat. "Well, of course, it is perfectly understood that ladies do not fully understand how money should be handled. It is why men run the world, after all. And," he added with emphasis, "why you come to us for assistance with whatever good works you wish to spend your time on." He pulled out his pocket watch and consulted it. "This has been an interesting interlude, but I have an important appointment. Ladies," he inclined his head.

The two gentlemen sitting in the front row joined him as he left the room. Mrs. Augustus, looking a little flustered, cast a troubled glance at his retreating back before rising to her feet.

"Thank you for your attendance today. I declare this meeting closed. Afternoon tea is ready at the back of the room. Please help yourselves."

Another round of applause resonated before the scrape of chairs and chatter took over. Emma and Henrietta joined the queue at the back of the room to collect their afternoon tea. The woman in front of Emma was in animated conversation with her companion, turning her head repeatedly. Every time she did, the long green feather on her hat threatened to tickle Emma's nose. As it swept past her face again, she took a half step back to avoid it.

"Ouch."

Emma turned and found herself facing a young woman, her face screwed up in pain.

Emma was mortified. "I am so dreadfully sorry. Did I step on your foot?"

"You did."

"I do apologise. I was trying to avoid the feather on that lady's hat in front of us."

"Mama," the young woman said. She raised her voice. "Mama."

The woman with the hat turned, causing Emma to twitch her head to avoid the feather once more. "What is it?"

"Honestly. I told you that hat was too much for today. You should keep it for race meetings if you must wear it at all. No one wants a feather in their face when they're having a cup of tea."

"Oh, really Delia. It's just a feather."

"Which has given me a bruise on my foot."

"Don't be silly."

"Delia's right, Gloria," the woman's companion told her. "That hat is dangerous. Hello, Mrs. Pickles, how are you?"

Henrietta, who had been trying not to laugh at the exchange, returned the greeting. "Have you met Mrs. Emma Berry?" she asked. "Her husband is Captain Daniel Berry of the PS *Mary B.*"

"No, but I'm very happy to meet her. Anyone who can shut up Henry Collins is a friend of mine. How do you do, Mrs. Berry? I'm Angela Wrightson. And this lady with the feather in her cap is Gloria Rasmussen."

Mrs. Rasmussen turned and nodded to Emma, her sharp dark eyes taking her in at a glance. Emma was glad she had chosen to wear her new plum-coloured suit with matching hat, the colour highlighting her green eyes. Mrs. Rasmussen's outfit was also very up to date, though with more frills and flounces, and clearly expensive.

"You may have shut him up," Mrs. Rasmussen told her, in no uncertain tone, "but he won't have gone away or forgotten about you. He's very powerful, you know, whatever we might think of him personally. The Society needs the support of his kind if we are to be of any use. We really can't have our members causing friction."

"Of course not," Emma murmured, feeling she'd been very clearly put in her place.

Angela Wrightson glanced between her friend and Emma but didn't disagree with what Mrs. Rasmussen had said. Henrietta reached out and squeezed her hand but also remained silent.

As they moved up in the queue, Emma's thoughts wandered to what she needed to do next day. Daniel would be home later in the afternoon. She mustn't forget to collect his new shirts from the seamstress when she did her shopping in the morning. Janey was cooking a roast lamb for dinner. Had she ordered enough potatoes when she'd placed this week's order with Ah Sing? Daniel loved roast potatoes.

"Emma?"

"Hmm?"

"Miss Rasmussen asked you a question," Henrietta told her.

"Oh. My apologies," Emma said, turning back to the young woman. "My mind was elsewhere."

"That's quite alright, Mrs. Berry," Delia said. "I was just saying that I haven't seen you at our meetings before. Are you a member?"

"No, not yet anyway. Henrietta, Mrs. Pickles, invited me along today."

"I do hope you join," Delia encouraged. "We can always do with more members, and you certainly rallied everyone after what that dreadful man had to say. My mother's opinion is not universal, you know."

"I will give it some thought," Emma told her.

Unfortunately, she was afraid Gloria Rasmussen's opinion may be held in higher esteem than her daughter imagined and would hold some sway in whom the Society accepted as a member. Mrs. Rasmussen's friend didn't disagree with what she'd said, after all. Pity her mind hadn't been wandering while Henry Collins was making his speech.

"You know," Delia said, leaning closer, "he isn't the mover and shaker he likes to think."

"No?"

"No, but I mustn't say more. Mrs. Augustus does a very good job, but she must walk a tightrope, keeping the Society on track while at the same time sweet talking everyone of influence to keep the donations coming in."

Chapter 2

Lunch at the Tearoom

"I WONDER WHAT young Delia meant with that comment about Mr. Collins," Henrietta mused, as she and Emma made their way up High Street on foot. "Her father is the Rasmussen of Kentish, Rasmussen and Foyle, the attorneys in Heygarth Street. I imagine what they don't know about the businessmen in town isn't worth knowing."

"Mmm?"

"Is something bothering you, Emma?" Henrietta asked. "You seem to be particularly preoccupied lately. If there's anything I can do to help, I'm always here if you need someone to talk to. Whatever you discuss with me won't go any further, you do know that don't you? I'm the soul of discretion when it comes to my friends."

Dear Henrietta. Emma had never been close to her own mother, although her relationship with Rose Haythorne had improved in recent years. She had always been close to her grandmother, but Eleanor had died three years ago, her famous herbal remedies unable to stop the decline of old age.

"Thank you, I very much appreciate your friendship," Emma told her. "I don't know what's wrong with me lately. I seem to drift off into daydreams at the drop of a hat."

It was extremely mortifying. Had she missed anyone else addressing her? If she failed to acknowledge people when they spoke to her, they would feel she thought herself above them, and they would be alienated before she even knew about it. She shuddered at the thought.

Henrietta put a calming hand on her arm, as they stopped to let a carrier's wagon turn into the main thoroughfare from Leslie Street. "You're at a loose end, Emma. You need to find something to focus on, some purpose."

"Isn't being a married woman with a child enough?"

Henrietta laughed, taking her arm as they walked on. "Some women could make that the sole purpose in their life, yes. Managing the home, the children, the husband. Involving themselves in good works. But not everyone. Not you. Or me. You need to find something for yourself. You had that on the riverboat, whether you realised it or not."

They'd reached the Primrose Tearoom, a low, wide building tucked between two double-storey red-brick buildings, one housing the Bank of Victoria, and the other, the Shamrock Hotel.

"Give it some thought," Henrietta advised.

"I will. Say hello to Janet for me. I'll come in for lunch tomorrow while I'm doing my weekly shop."

They parted company and Emma hurried off to meet Darcy at the Grammar School. It was on Dickson Street, the northern end of High Street, on the far side of Hopwood Square and almost opposite the new police station. Although their home on Watson Street was only a block and half away, Emma liked to be there to meet Darcy when school let out, and he always seemed pleased to see her.

They were both looking forward to Daniel's arrival tomorrow, and spending time with him before he steamed away again. She missed his companionship since she'd stopped travelling on the *Mary B*, but at age seven, Darcy needed formal schooling, and the thought of sending him away to boarding school at that young age had not sat well with her, even without considering the cost.

As she walked, she pondered on what Henrietta had said, and what purpose she could possibly carve out for herself here in town. Making up herbal remedies was the only real skill she had, and with three doctors in town there was little call for that, although she did still supply some herbals for stations downriver. Of course, she also had some experience in solving suspicious deaths, but one couldn't make a career out of murder, could they.

EMMA PUSHED open the door to the Primrose Tearoom at lunch time next day. Henrietta had updated the decor several times since she first visited the place, a decade ago. The walls were still painted a soft blue but gone were the floral curtains and red gingham tablecloths. The tables were now covered in a plain dark blue and the curtains were striped, blue, yellow, and white. It still showed Henrietta's eclectic taste, but with a more elegant touch.

Today, the Primrose was busy with ladies taking their midday lunch, many with bags of shopping on the floor beside their chairs. Janet greeted Emma and Janey from behind the counter where she was dealing with a customer.

Her friend had put on a little weight since having her two children, but she was still pretty, with a high forehead, and dark hair in a soft arrangement, loosely pinned at the back. She was wearing her usual work uniform of a white pinafore over a simple grey dress. Janet and Henrietta looked alike, definitely a mother-daughter duo, but Henrietta favoured a more severe look with her hair pulled back into a low bun.

"There's a table available down the side," Janet told her. "I'll be over in a minute to take your order."

Emma smiled and thanked her. Several ladies nodded as she crossed the room, and she returned the greeting, vaguely recognising their faces. They must have been at the Society's meeting yesterday.

There was also the odd glance at Janey, but that wasn't unusual. Not many ladies took lunch with their maid, especially a dark skinned one. Emma knew she would be considered odd in that respect. She could only hope people would accept it eventually, even if they did think her more than a trifle eccentric. She still thanked her lucky stars that Janey and Abe had moved to Echuca with her. It had been like bringing a piece of Wirramilla with her.

They tucked their shopping bags out of the way against the wall and took their seats. A light lunch was in order, with the promise of a roast dinner later.

"I'll just have the tomato soup and a sandwich, with tea," Emma decided.

Janey nodded. "Me too. And a scone?" Even Janey admired Henrietta's light fruit scones.

"Alright, and a scone," Emma agreed.

She glanced up as Old Mr. Pickles passed their table to take his seat at the one by the window with the single chair. His table. As he removed his hat, Emma couldn't help but notice how frail he was looking. His white hair had thinned, showing the pink scalp beneath, and there were dark circles under his eyes. She supposed he must be around eighty years old.

Certainly, his children, Nathaniel and Charity, had to be in their late forties.

He was wearing a woollen coat too, which surprised her on such a mild day, and while he did unbutton it, his fingers shaky and fumbling, he didn't take it off. Her observations were interrupted by Janet's arrival at their table.

"Is Daniel home yet?" Janet asked after taking their order.

"He's due later today," Emma replied. "How is Alex, and how are the children?" It had been at least three days since they'd spoken.

Janet rolled her eyes. "Alex has taken Colin with him to the livery stable today. Winnie doesn't seem able to manage him at all. If you hear of someone else looking for a nanny's job, do let me know. Please."

Emma said she would, though she had no idea if she could help at all. She also wasn't sure the livery stable was the best place for an active five-year-old either. Janet turned to leave, but not before hesitating and casting a look at her grandfather. Emma couldn't see her face, but she saw Janey frown before Janet hurried off to see to their lunch order.

"What is it?" Emma asked.

"Somethin's bothering her."

"She just said she's having trouble with the nanny."

"No. Something about him." Janey indicated with her head in the direction of Old Mr. Pickles.

"Well, that's hardly surprising. He's not looking well."

"So, why didn't she go speak to him?"

"Probably because she knew he wouldn't want to be fussed over," Emma replied.

Old Mr. Pickles was a reserved, austere man. Emma had reason to feel grateful to him for one occasion years ago, but she'd only seen him in passing since settling in town. He'd never acknowledged her, and she doubted he remembered her from her time as a temporary resident at the boarding house. His daughter Charity certainly remembered.

She realised Janey had that baleful look on her face when she felt she knew better.

"Have you heard something?" Emma asked now. She didn't need Janey to get uppity. She needed a peaceful and smoothly run home for the next few days at least.

"His other daughter is visitin'," Janey said.

"Yes, Henrietta told me. Grace, I believe her name is."

She hadn't met the woman, but Janet had spoken of her aunt, who was recently widowed. She wondered if Grace's name fitted her better than Charity's did. Grace's daughter and fiancé were visiting as well. Surely having her cousin visit hadn't put Janet out of sorts with her grandfather, but who knew what really went on in other families. There were enough undercurrents in her own.

Henrietta delivered their lunch but didn't linger beyond their usual exchange of greetings. The Tearoom was busy. She heard a grunted 'thank you' from Old Mr. Pickles as the waitress, Alice, delivered his meal.

Lunch was a pleasant respite, but it was time they were getting on home. She hoped Abe had finished painting the hall. She wanted Daniel to be able to relax and enjoy his family when he was at home and not have busywork going on around him. Her decision to take Darcy and leave the *Mary B* had not been without its issues.

As Emma was paying her bill, Old Mr. Pickles left the Tearoom. She and Janey were about to follow him out when she noticed he'd stopped right outside and was speaking to someone. It was Henry Collins. She didn't want to encounter the man.

She turned back abruptly, bumping into Janey and causing her to drop the bag of groceries she was carrying. A green bottle of Worcestershire Sauce and several packets of barley spilled out. Fortunately, nothing burst open. As Janey bent to pick them up, Emma pretended to consider the items in the display cabinet on the counter, as if the mishap with the shopping had nothing to do with her.

"Did you want something?" Janet asked.

Emma glanced over her shoulder. The men were still there. "I'm trying to avoid someone."

"Grandfather? Why would you want to avoid my grandfather?"

"No, Henry Collins. Tell me when he's gone."

Janet giggled, her brown eyes crinkling. "What have you been up to?"

"Ask your mother."

"Oh, I will," she said, as Emma continued to stare at the display of cakes. "Are you sure you wouldn't like something? Mother's apple sponge is particularly nice. Very moist, and only three pence a slice."

"Huh," Janey huffed from behind.

Emma raised her eyebrows at Janet. Her friend knew only too well what Janey's reaction would be if she bought cake from the Tearoom, or from anywhere for that matter. Mutiny, at best.

"Has he gone yet?" she asked Janet pointedly.

Janet giggled again. "Coast's clear," she said, and turned to deal with another customer, who was looking at Emma a trifle oddly.

Outside, she saw Henry Collins and Old Mr. Pickles walking up the street together. She and Janey turned in the opposite direction where they hired Mr. Crowley's hansom cab standing right next door in front of the Shamrock Hotel. They didn't have Abe to carry the shopping for them today.

As they rolled down the street, Emma wondered what connection Henry Collins had with Old Mr. Pickles. Collins had looked annoyed when he spoke to the older man. She wouldn't have given them much thought except for Delia Rasmussen's comment yesterday.

◇◇◇

EMMA WAS relieved to see the painting of the hallway had been completed when she and Janey reached home. Abe had excelled himself. He'd started last evening and was at it again before they'd left for town, which was probably why he was asleep now on the front verandah. Janey kicked at his leg to wake him.

"Hey," he protested. "Where's me lunch? I'm starvin'."

"You can make a sandwich," Janey countered.

"A sandwich!"

Emma left them to their chivvying and surveyed the hall, admiring its freshness. The smoky yellow ceiling was now a pristine white, and the walls pale blue, the colour achieved by adding washing blue to the whitewash mixture. It was a time-consuming job, as the whitewash had to be made up every hour and put on quickly. Abe had done well. But it made the other rooms look drab by comparison.

She went to her storage cupboard in the spare bedroom and searched through a box of candles for what she wanted. Lemon verbena. If the whole house wasn't freshly painted it could at least smell fresh, and what better scent for that than a citrusy one? Two candles in the hall, another in the parlour, and one in their bedroom would do.

That done, she took her personal shopping to the bedroom, leaving Janey and Abe in the kitchen quietly talking as the scent of pancakes and bacon drifted through the house. At least Janey was talking, no doubt telling Abe about their morning.

She unpacked Daniel's new shirts and placed them neatly folded in his drawer. She'd found a frayed thread on the cuff of one three weeks ago. She wasn't having her riverboat captain looking anything but smart. His old shirts would go to the seamstress next week for new cuffs and collars. There was plenty of wear still in the body. She twitched the corner of the quilt and plumped up a pillow.

In the kitchen, Abe was wiping the last of the golden syrup off his plate with a finger. He was about to put it in his mouth but picked up the napkin, lying clean and pristine beside his plate instead, when Emma walked in.

Chapter 3

Called Away

"COULD YOU MAKE sure the verandahs are swept," Emma told Abe, sorry for depriving him of that last sweet mouthful but there were more important things to be doing right now.

"Uh-huh."

"And make sure all the tools are back in the shed, and the paint things cleaned and put away."

"Uh-huh."

"And if…"

"Emma, stop," Janey interrupted. "We do this every time. Here," she handed Emma the potato peeler. There was a basket of fresh vegetables on the kitchen counter. Ah Sing had delivered their order while they were out, and there were the extra potatoes. She supposed she could at least be trusted to peel the potatoes and carrots for their roast dinner.

She counted it a luxury to have a market garden only a few streets over, by the Campaspe River. Ah Sing worked it with an older Chinese man, and Ah

Lo, the *Mary B*'s cook, when he was at home. Ah Lo would stock the *Mary B's* galley with vegetables at the beginning of a trip, and Lucy would be sure to restock it at Wirramilla, on their way back. Bacon, eggs, lamb chops. and juicy steak were what the crew wanted, but they got fresh vegetables too. Emma hadn't heard any complaints.

Abe disappeared to do whatever he considered needed doing, and an hour later Emma decided she had time for a cup of tea before meeting Darcy at school. She was planning to take him to the wharf and stay there a while. There was a chance the *Mary B* would come in while they waited. She stirred the fire under the kettle and sat at the table to wait for it to boil.

She knew she should be used to it by now, but there was a drowning last week when a laden barge overturned, trapping the pilot. These accidents hadn't caused her as much worry when she was on the river herself, on the spot. Henrietta was right. She needed something to fill her time, and her mind.

Janey put a plate with slices of orange cake on the table. She didn't need cake so soon after lunch but imagined Janey might be making a point. Abe, who seemed to have a sixth sense when tea was brewing, appeared from the rooms he shared with Janey off the side of the kitchen. He waited until Janey had sat down with the teapot before joining them at the table. It wasn't a matter of good manners. He simply wasn't comfortable sitting there if it was just Emma at the table. It had taken him a long time to get to the point of sitting down at all.

Emma took a sip of her tea and tried to relax, gazing out the window at the front garden, the view framed by the white net curtains. The plumbago hedge along the front fence sported its permanent display of blue blossoms, just like the hedge around the homestead at Wirramilla. Brightening the entrance with their pinks, reds and whites were the vincas, lining both sides of the path to the front door.

The dining nook came a close second to the back verandah as her favourite spot to sit. Because the house had been built facing the river, the kitchen, usually at the back of a house, was on the street frontage.

When Daniel had initially bought and renovated the house, he'd had the kitchen extended out to the edge of the front verandah, creating the dining nook and a more appropriate 'front room' space. It had been Henrietta's suggestion, before Emma even knew Daniel had bought the place for them, or that he was intending to propose.

"Emma?" Janey was wiggling her fingers to get her attention.

"Mmmh?"

"Abe asked if you was still going to make that liniment oil Friday?" Emma stared at the girl for a moment, unable to process what she was saying. "You've forgot, haven't you?"

She had. She didn't miss the look Janey and Abe exchanged. Apparently, her absentmindedness had become a topic of discussion. This was getting to be a real worry.

Had she made a mistake when she decided to leave the *Mary B*? But she'd had to. She couldn't have Darcy growing up barely literate amongst a bunch of rough men, no matter how goodhearted they were.

"Um, yes, yes, of course, I'll be making it."

"I'll get everythin' ready," Abe told her. He needed to get a stack of wood for the outdoor fireplace, and wash out the witch's cauldron, as Janey called it.

Eleanor Haythorne's recipe for liniment oil was popular among the pastoralists and their men for relieving the strains and sprains they were often subject too, and they needed her to keep them supplied now, just as her grandmother had done.

Daniel planned to spend Friday with Darcy. Their son didn't know yet that he was getting the day off school for that treat. It didn't pay to tell him before it was a certainty.

The sound of a horse and carriage approaching at a clip caught their attention. Janey half stood and peered out the window.

"It's Mr. Crowley," she said.

"Did we leave a bag of shopping in the cab?" Emma asked. She didn't feel she could trust herself with anything right now.

"Nope. It's all here."

The horse drawn cab pulled up in front of their house. Had the *Mary B* already arrived, and Daniel taken a cab home? It was unlike him, unless he was bringing something that was too heavy to carry all the way, but then he would have just dropped it off on his way to the wharf.

"Mr. Crowley's getting down," Janey said.

Abe got to his feet and went out to meet him. A moment later he came quickly back in.

"He says it's urgent. Mrs. Pickles wants you to come right away," he told Emma.

"Did he say what it was about?" she asked, getting up from her seat and leaving just the crumbs of the cake she hadn't needed. Abe shook his head. "Can you meet Darcy at school? Take him to the wharf and I'll try to join you there as soon as I can. I could drop you on the way."

"You've no time, and we've lots," Janey told her, handing Emma her bag.

Emma had the suspicion it wouldn't just be Abe collecting Darcy and visiting the wharf. "Don't forget, you need to get the roast in the oven."

"I haven't forgotten anything," Janey told her.

Emma didn't miss the emphasis on the first word. She went out to the waiting cab where Mr. Crowley was holding the door for her.

"Why does Henrietta need me, do you know?" she asked.

Mr. Crowley's jowls wobbled as he shook his grey head. "No, ma'am. Just that we were to hurry." He closed the door behind her and hauled himself back up onto his seat.

Emma found herself rocked and jolted as Mr. Crowley urged his horse along Dickson Street at a fast trot. She hadn't asked, but had expected they were going to the Tearoom, and was surprised when Mr. Crowley took the cab around the corner into Connelly Street.

Something was wrong at the Pickles' Boarding House? Emma's imagination was racing overtime. Was someone ill? Had there been an accident?

The Pickles' attractive two-storey brick house didn't appear to have changed at all since she'd stayed there a decade ago. Some of the shrubs in the small front garden needed pruning, and the gate squeaked as she opened it. The sound must have been heard inside, as Henrietta had opened the front door before Emma reached it.

"Emma, thank you so much for coming. I know you're expecting Daniel, but I'm so frightened."

"My dear, what has happened?" She could hear voices coming from the parlour. And someone sobbing.

"My father-in-law has died."

Emma remembered how unwell he had looked at the Tearoom.

"Was it a heart attack?"

"If only."

"Henrietta, you're frightening me now. What is it?"

"He may have been hit on the head."

"Oh, but..."

"You killed him," a woman's distraught voice came clearly from the parlour. Another female voice responded. Was that Janet? Emma couldn't make out the words.

"Who is it making that accusation?"

"That's Miriam, Grace's daughter," Henrietta said. "You'd best come and see for yourself."

She stepped down the hall and pushed the parlour door wide open. Emma reluctantly followed her inside, wondering again what she was doing here.

Conversations ceased as all heads turned toward them. The first thing Emma noticed was the heat. Despite the mild weather, there was a fire burning in the fireplace. Drawn up in front of it was a wing-backed armchair. She could just see the side of a man's white head, slumped against the back.

A young woman Emma hadn't seen before was kneeling beside the chair, her head on her hands as they rested on the armrest. She had dark brown ringlets falling around her face and was wearing white muslin sprigged with pink. The young man stooping over her, a hand on her shoulder, was tall, slim, and blonde haired.

A very romantic picture. Emma could almost suppose it was posed. They must be Miriam, the visiting granddaughter, and her fiancé.

Charity Pickles was sitting on the sofa, her hands clutched tightly in her lap, a slip of a white handkerchief protruding between two fingers, her thin grey face even sharper than usual. As always, she wore black, unrelieved with any touch of white, as if she were forever in mourning.

A slightly younger woman, whose similar features had a softer look than Charity's, was standing on the opposite side of the fireplace. She too, was dressed in black, but Emma knew the other Pickles daughter, Grace, was a widow. While her demeanour was calm and composed, she emitted an undercurrent of sadness.

Standing in the centre of the room with Janet, was her father Nathaniel Pickles, Henrietta's estranged husband, an austere man, like his father, with an only slightly warmer personality, but a wry sense of humour. Their faces were etched with shock and disbelief.

"What is she doing here?" Charity's harsh voice broke the moment of silence that had greeted Emma's appearance. "Sticking your nose in again, are you?" she asked, looking to Emma and not waiting for Henrietta to reply.

"I want her here, Aunt Charity," Janet said, sending a tremulous glance at Emma.

"You never were very discerning when it came to your friends," Charity sniffed.

"Please, Charity, this isn't a time for arguing among ourselves," Grace said, a pleading note in her voice.

"What would you know?" Charity's head snapped around to glare at her sister. "You've barely been in the place five minutes."

"Now, now," Nathaniel put in, ineffectively, as Charity went on as if he hadn't spoken.

"This is my home, not yours. You left, remember."

"A woman usually does leave her parents' home when she marries," Grace retorted.

"And who's fault is it that I didn't?" Charity sniped back.

"Stop it, both of you," Janet cried. "How can you talk like that when grandfather is, is…"

"But you killed him," Miriam accused, looking up quickly, her voice shrill. "You were standing right here with a piece of firewood in your hand. I practically caught her in the act," she said, looking around. "Oh, if only I'd been a few minutes earlier, I could have stopped her."

"The firewood was lying on the floor," Janet cried. "I keep telling you, I'd just picked it up. I thought Grandfather was asleep."

Henrietta glanced at Emma, eyebrows raised as if to say, 'see why I need your help?' Surely Henrietta wasn't expecting her to step in and sort this out?

A loud rat, tat on the front door drew everyone's attention.

"What now?" Charity asked.

The fiancé cleared his throat. "I sent for the doctor, and the police," he said.

"The police?"

There were voices in the hall and the Pickles' maid ushered in a man in his mid-twenties, with brown eyes in a fresh face, and a small moustache like a furry caterpillar above his upper lip. It had been grown to make himself look older and more professional was Emma's first thought. It didn't quite work.

"Doctor Rook," the maid announced.

"Where's Dr. MacArthur?" Charity demanded.

"He's been called out," Doctor Rook told her. "Now, what seems to be the problem. The message I received was rather confusing."

"My father-in-law has died," Henrietta said, indicating the armchair. "We need to know the cause of death."

"We know how he died," Miriam countered. "He's been murdered."

Doctor Rook's eyes widened.

"We heard you the first three times, miss," Charity said, "so do be quiet, now. Move away and let the doctor do his job."

"Oh."

Emma found herself agreeing with Charity Pickles for perhaps the first time since she'd known the woman. Doctor Rook stepped toward his patient, and Miriam's young man, whose name Emma still didn't know, drew her to her feet and away to the side.

Emma hadn't met Doctor Rook, or any of the doctors in town, though she knew of Dr. MacArthur. If you read everything in the newspapers about deaths, murder trials, and the latest developments in medicine, as she did, you knew the major people involved. Dr. MacArthur was also the coroner.

If there was doubt as to how Mr. Pickles had died, she expected the coroner would order an autopsy. But would this young doctor consider that, or make his own diagnosis? Emma thought it wouldn't hurt to make some subtle observations of her own.

Chapter 4

Janet Under Suspicion

AS DOCTOR ROOK bent to examine the body, Emma stepped around to the far side of the armchair where Old Mr. Pickles sat, earning a hiss from Charity. She crouched down to get a better view. It was the first chance she'd had to see the old man clearly. His open eyes took her aback for a moment, staring but not seeing.

"A heart attack, do you think, Doctor?" she asked, barely above a whisper.

He gave her a startled look. "I don't think…"

"Someone is claiming he was hit on the head."

Doctor Rook peered at the side of Mr. Pickles head that was exposed to view. He parted the thin hair with long, delicate fingers, before crouching down and looking at the face more closely once again.

"There appears to be an abrasion, but virtually no blood," he said thoughtfully.

Emma drew in a sharp breath. "Isn't that unusual? Head wounds tend to bleed profusely, don't they?"

She knew perfectly well they did, but deferring to him would do no harm.

"Have you medical experience, Miss, er, Mrs..? he asked.

"Mrs. Emma Berry. I'm a herbalist by training, but I have seen a few deaths in my lifetime."

"Er, yes, of course."

Emma almost wanted to assure him that she hadn't caused any of them herself. "Could he have fallen, do you think?"

"What?"

"The abrasion to the head. Could he have fallen, hit his head, got back in his chair, and then had a heart attack? He is quite elderly. I thought, when I saw him earlier today, that he didn't look very well."

"You spoke to him today?"

"We didn't speak. He was having lunch at the Tearoom when I was there."

"And what time was that?"

"A little after twelve."

Doctor Rook lifted the right hand that was hanging loosely over the arm of the chair and flexed the fingers.

"The room is very warm," Emma mused, almost to herself.

"Why are you two whispering?" Charity demanded. "What are you cooking up?"

"I beg your pardon, madam?" Doctor Rook stood and stared at Charity, his tone clearly betraying his outrage at her comment.

"Not you. Her."

Emma got to her feet as the doctor turned a questioning look her way. At least he had some backbone, standing up to Charity Pickles, but she wasn't done yet.

"The matter of lividity would still come into play regardless of temperature, wouldn't it, Doctor?" she asked, a little desperately.

"Of course."

"And digestion of food?"

"Indeed."

The look he gave her this time suggested he thought her a distinctly odd woman. Emma hoped she wasn't overdoing it, but as she opened her mouth to speak again, Charity got in before her.

"Well? Was my father murdered, or did he die of a heart attack?"

"I cannot be certain from the evidence to hand," Doctor Rook replied. "Several factors need further investigation. I will have to discuss the matter with Dr. MacArthur, but it's likely it will require an autopsy to determine cause of death."

"You're cutting him up?" Grace cried in horror, her hands going to her face.

Miriam fainted into the arms of her fiancé, as Emma breathed a sigh of relief. It was at that moment the police arrived, in the form of one Sergeant Thomas Donovan.

"So, we have a dead man with a wound to the back of his head, and a witness who saw a person by the body with a lump of firewood in her hand."

Sergeant Donovan had very quickly gotten to the gist of the story, despite the undercurrents in the room, not least of which concerned his own Irish heritage.

Emma hadn't met him before, but she'd seen him pacing the streets in his very British bobby's uniform, complete with helmet. He was an imposing figure, tall and muscular, with a full beard and bushy moustache. She couldn't imagine him standing for any nonsense.

"That's your story, is it then?" he asked, turning his piercing blue-eyed gaze on Miriam.

Miriam was struggling under his questioning. She hesitated for a moment, as if suddenly realising the significance of what she was claiming. Then she nodded.

"Yes. Yes," she repeated more strongly.

"So where is this piece of firewood?"

"I think I dropped it in the basket," Janet replied, pointing to the large wicker basket tucked beside the fireplace.

Sergeant Donovan stepped forward and peered into it. Then he picked up the basket with one hand and tipped it over. It was empty.

"Are you sure you didn't put it on the fire?"

"I'm sure I didn't."

"Why is it I shouldn't arrest you for the murder of your grandfather?" he asked, as he dropped the wicker basket to the floor.

Janet seemed to shrink, trying to disappear behind her father, who put his arm around her shoulder in a display of support and affection that Emma hadn't expected of Nathaniel Pickles. It seemed to surprise Janet a little too.

"She told you the firewood was on the floor, and she'd just picked it up when Miriam came into the room," Nathaniel said. "Besides, what possible motive could she have?"

"They argued," Miriam said.

"If people were to kill everyone they argued with, this world would have half as many people in it," Sergeant Donovan put in drily. "Although that might not be such a bad idea, but for all that, what was this argument supposed to be about?"

What indeed, Emma wondered.

"Grandfather's will," Miriam replied.

"Is that right? Money is what it's about, is it?"

"No," Janet said. "Grandfather told us two days ago that he was leaving this house to me, but…"

"It's a complete travesty of justice," Charity cried. "I've worked my fingers to the bone running this place for the past thirty years, bringing in an income from guests. We'll challenge the will. Father clearly wasn't in his right mind when he wrote it. This house should pass to the three of us, father's children. This is my home."

"And mine," Nathaniel put in.

"Indeed," Grace agreed.

"Of course it should," Janet said loudly. "I don't want the house. I've got a home of my own already. I told Grandfather that. It's what we were arguing about after he'd told us."

"Oh, a likely story," Miriam said. "As if anyone would turn down owning this house. It's more likely you killed him because he'd told you he was changing his will and was going to write you out. That's why you came sneaking in here isn't it?

"I didn't sneak in," Janet said hotly. "He sent me a note asking me to call."

"He sent you a note, did he?" Sergeant Donovan asked.

"Yes, that's why I was here," Janet said. "He asked me to come and see him at once."

"Can I see this note?" the Sergeant asked.

"It's on the tea table."

All eyes pivoted to the tea table. Apart from a neat pile of magazines and a folded newspaper, there was no note of any sort in view. Sergeant Donovan spent several minutes moving and shaking out the magazines and the papers. The table was in a mess but there was no note.

"Are you sure you put it here?" he asked at last, clearly disbelieving.

"Yes."

"Why?"

"Why? Because it's, it's what I always did. Grandfather didn't like waste. He would have used the piece that wasn't written on or used the other side. He would have expected me to return it."

Sergeant Donovan didn't look convinced.

"She's right," Charity said, reluctantly it seemed to Emma. "My father was very pernickety about such things. You saw how neatly everything was arranged on the table. He didn't tolerate waste or mess."

The Sergeant sighed. "Right, so what did this note say, as accurately as you can remember?"

Janet took a breath. "I need to speak to you. Come at once. Grandfather."

Emma saw Nathaniel frown. Did he not believe his daughter had received a note?

"And what did he have to say?" Sergeant Donovan said.

"I don't know," Janet cried, all but wringing her hands. "He was dead already."

"You knew he was dead?"

"No. I thought he was asleep. Miriam said he was dead. I told you that. She checked on him when he didn't answer her, and she started screaming at me and accusing me of killing him. I didn't. I didn't kill him."

Sergeant Donovan ticked items off his fingers. "The firewood he appears to have been hit with is missing. The note you say he sent you is missing. Did you throw them both in the fire?"

"No, I've told you what happened. I don't know why the note isn't there. I put it on the table."

"Just like you put the firewood in the basket, I suppose."

"I thought I had," Janet said, close to breaking.

"We need the results of the autopsy," Emma said, before they got into another round of accusations. "It isn't clear what happened here yet."

Sergeant Donovan's blue eyes glittered as he turned his gaze on her.

"Mrs. Berry it is, I believe," he said. "I heard you'd retired from meddling in police business." Emma's eyes widened. He knew who she was? And her past?

"What do you say, Doctor?" he asked turning to Doctor Rook. "Is it an autopsy we're needing?"

"I would advise it being the wiser course," Doctor Rook replied. "But of course, that will be for Dr. MacArthur's to decide. He is the coroner after all."

"Well, then, we'd best get himself down to the surgery as soon as possible. Would you arrange for the coroner's wagon then, Doctor?"

"Certainly. I'll do it at once." Doctor Rook left, and Sergeant Donovan said he would wait out front for the wagon to arrive. He might have thought of allowing them some privacy to take their final leave of their family member, but there was no such fine feeling evident among those still in the room.

"What a disaster," Grace bemoaned. "At least while Father was alive, we had a chance of getting him to rethink his will. This is dreadful. I don't know what I'm going to do now."

Charity huffed as the clock on the mantle struck five. "Dinner will be late. At least the kitchen is still mine. For the moment."

Nathaniel appeared bewildered. "It's a mess, indeed," he said. "For all his care, all his life, he's managed to leave a mess behind at the last moment."

"I didn't kill him," Janet whispered. Miriam shot her a venomous look but had the sense not to say anything.

Poor Old Mr. Pickles. Not a tear shed. Emma felt out of place and unable to think of anything that would help the situation.

"I need to go," she said to Henrietta. "Daniel's arriving tonight. He may be home already."

"I doubt it, Mrs. Berry," Nathaniel said. "He's been held up with a broken paddle strut. We received a telegraph from Perricoota just before I was called home."

As the senior clerk at the wharf office, Nathaniel Pickles knew everything that went on along the river concerning the riverboats. Captains were required to update their schedules whenever they were able.

"Oh. Thank you for that information," Emma told him, feeling deflated. Henrietta cast her a sympathetic glance.

"I'd walk back with you, but I need to see Janet home," Henrietta told her.

"Of course, you do."

Nathaniel walked out to the front gate with the three of them, passing Sergeant Donovan who was lounging in a chair on the verandah.

"What do you think the autopsy will reveal?" Nathaniel asked Emma.

"I'm hoping it will establish time of death, at the very least," Emma replied, hoping the Sergeant wasn't listening, but knowing he would be.

"Yes." Nathaniel didn't sound confident.

Emma was about to ask what had troubled him about the note Janet claimed to have received from her grandfather, when the jingle of harness drew their attention. Mr. Crowley's hansom cab pulled up.

"Mrs. Berry, I've just seen a very disappointed boy and his friends walking home from the wharf," Mr. Crowley said, looking down from his seat. "I suspect he could do with his mama about now. Can I offer you a lift?"

Emma suddenly realised how much she longed to be home, compounded by the disappointment of Daniel's delayed arrival. "Thank you," she told him, and promised Janet and Henrietta she would see them next day.

As Mr. Crowley drove her away, she saw Nathaniel offer his arm to Henrietta, who took it, her other hand around Janet's shoulder as they started down the street. Emma didn't know what had caused the Pickles' estrangement, which was longstanding, but her heart warmed to Nathaniel. His support tonight was more than just politeness.

"Is everything all right in Connelly Street?" Mr. Crowley asked as he held the cab door for Emma to alight outside her home. She should have guessed her ride had come with the price of information. He was getting too old to get up and down from his seat to open the door for his passengers.

"I'm afraid not, Mr. Crowley. Old Mr. Pickles died this afternoon."

"Ah, I was afraid it might be something like that. I'm sure your friends needed you to provide comfort."

"What little I could," Emma told him.

She knew he suspected there was more to it, especially with the Sergeant sitting on the front verandah for all the world to see. Whatever news was broadcast on the morrow would only confirm that suspicion. Because even should it turn out to have been a heart attack that killed him, who had hit Old Mr. Pickles on the head? And why? Because she didn't believe for one moment that it was Janet.

Chapter 5

Janey Has a Suggestion

THE FAIRY WRENS chittered above in the eucalypts as Emma sat on the back verandah overlooking the river. The roast lamb that Daniel would be too late home to eat was filling the house with its meaty aroma.

Below her, Darcy, and his friend, Jemmy, were catching water striders and tadpoles at the river's edge. Or trying to. It seemed to Emma they were having more fun just getting wet and dirty. Jemmy's mother would not be impressed. Fortunately, Emma had suggested he stay for dinner to keep Darcy occupied, so there would be time for him to get cleaned up and dried off before Abe escorted him around the corner to his home later.

Janey appeared carrying a bowl and a small saucepan. She tipped a generous number of pea pods from the bowl into Emma's lap. The pan she placed on the bench between them as she sat and began to shell the peas from the bowl. Emma picked up a fat pea pod from her lap and popped it open. Neither spoke for a few minutes.

"She'd never have done something like that," Janey said, peas plinking into the empty pan.

"No." But something had been wrong. They'd seen it themselves, at the Tearoom.

"You going to sort it out?"

"I don't know if there's anything to sort out yet." It would depend on the autopsy if the coroner took Dr. Rook's suggestion that one was necessary.

"Huh. Peggy would know what went on in that house."

"Peggy?"

"The maid."

Of course, servants knew everything. "Do you know her?" Emma reached for a fresh handful of pea pods from the bowl. She might have seen the girl about town and not known who she was.

"Haven't spoken to her. But I could." Emma wondered if Peggy was white. More than likely. She knew Janey had friends among the few coloured domestics in town.

"Let's wait and see what happens tomorrow." She wasn't in any hurry to get involved.

"Huh."

They finished shelling the peas. Janey took them inside to cook as the last rays of the sun slanted over the water, before winking out. The swallows had taken over the trees for the night. Their gentle murmuring could go on for hours. Emma had the fanciful idea they were discussing their day and what they were planning for tomorrow. The birds hadn't long returned from wintering in the north. She got to her feet, suddenly tired, and called the boys in to get cleaned up for dinner.

After Jemmy had gone home, Emma read to Darcy from a book of Grimm's fairy tales. She wasn't sure how much either of them took in of Rumpelstiltskin and his gold spinning, as their senses were tuned to the sound of a distinctive riverboat whistle, or footsteps on the verandah. Emma stopped reading when Darcy yawned for the second time.

"I want to wait up," he complained, when Emma suggested it was time he went to bed.

"You can get up again if you hear him come home," Emma promised, knowing what a sound sleeper he was. She ushered him into his bedroom. "Daddy will be here tomorrow. Think about that as you go to sleep. Tomorrow will come so-o much quicker."

Darcy hugged the stuffed koala Nella had made for him and closed his eyes tightly. Emma smiled as she kissed his forehead.

"Sweet dreams."

She sent Janey and Abe off to bed shortly after ten and remained sitting by the dying embers of the parlour fire in her night clothes. It wasn't that a fire was needed so much as it provided comfort. She'd already dozed off once and was about to take herself off to bed, as well, when she heard the welcome sound of a boat chugging slowly, growing closer, before sliding gently to rest below the house. It was after midnight. The tension she hadn't realised filled her body, dissipated.

Emma went out to the verandah, wrapper tightly fastened, to say a quiet greeting to the crew. They'd all elected to sleep on board at this hour. Daniel made sure the fire under the boiler was dampened before he left them to it.

"What a day," he told her, after releasing her from a warm hug and a kiss in the privacy of the hallway. "I was expecting to be home hours ago. Did you get the telegraph?" Emma told him she had as she followed him into the bedroom. "It was well after dark by the time we got the paddle repaired and then we had to take it easy. How is everyone, anyway," he asked, having got that off his chest. He was sitting on the edge of the bed, pulling off his boots.

Emma decided it would be time enough in the morning to tell him about Old Mr. Pickles. "We're all fine. Darcy will be excited to see you when he wakes up."

"I'm not going off again until Monday," he said, voice muffled as he pulled off his shirt.

Emma handed him a clean nightshirt. It was still only Wednesday, despite all that had happened, so they had four whole days. She hoped she would have them free. Daniel was already snoring by the time she blew out the candle and climbed into bed beside him.

EMMA WOKE next morning to the scent of bacon and eggs. It wasn't coming from her own kitchen though, but from the *Mary B.* Ah Lo was making sure the crew didn't leave on an empty stomach. It took a little longer for her and Daniel to have their own breakfast. Daniel had managed a cup of tea before walking Darcy to school.

The boy didn't want to go, but he had the promise of tomorrow off school to spend with his father, on condition he went today. Emma didn't envy his teachers. Finally, they were sitting in the dining nook, and Emma was able to tell Daniel about Old Mr. Pickles' death.

"I don't know how you get mixed up in these things," Daniel said. "Can't you leave it to the coroner and the police? It's their job after all."

Emma felt a surge of annoyance that died as soon as it appeared. She understood that Daniel's comment was fueled by his concern for her, unlike Henry Collins' criticism of the Ladies Benevolent Society, which stemmed from arrogance and a sense of superiority.

"I'm not involved in anything," she assured him. "I'm just an impartial observer."

"An observer? Impartial? Did you hear that, Janey?"

"I hear," Janey replied, as she put a plate of sausages and eggs in front of Daniel. Fortunately, she made no other comment, which was just as well, considering she'd been the one eager to ask questions last night. "More toast?" she asked Emma.

"Please." She was enjoying the fig jam Lucy had sent with Daniel. "You wouldn't expect me to sit by and see Janet charged with murder, would you? But there's nothing to do yet. It will depend on what the coroner has to say. It's just… I have a nasty feeling about this."

"Of course you do."

Emma decided to ignore the sarcasm, gentle as it was. "Do you remember that case a few years back where scraps of hair were found on a hammer, and led to the exhumation of a man's body?"

"I remember you talking about it at the time."

"It was all a bit odd. An inquest was held to discover whether he'd died from a blow to the head, or of natural causes. The wife claimed she couldn't wake him one morning and called for help. Whoever examined him at the time didn't find any injuries on the body, and he was declared to have died of the ill health he'd suffered for the previous two years."

Daniel nodded. "But someone thought it was suspicious, didn't they."

"They did. Samples of his hair matched those on a hammer found by the bed, and two doctors, including our Mr. MacArthur, declared he'd died from a blow to the head. The wife was convicted and is serving a life sentence in Melbourne Gaol." She shivered. It wasn't a fate she wanted for Janet.

"Do you think the verdict was wrong?

Emma shook her head. "I have no idea. The wife, if she did it, couldn't have been very bright, leaving the murder weapon lying there beside the bed for days. I've always wondered if someone else delivered the blow and left the murder weapon so it couldn't be linked to them. Without seeing any medical reports, I don't know what else the doctors discovered, or how well they examined the body."

"So, what are the parallels? Are you thinking old Pickles died from natural causes, or the blow to the head?"

"It could be either. The more I think about it, the time of death could be critical. I tried to put ideas into Doctor Rook's head about the things that needed looking into…"

"Oh, I've no doubt you did."

Emma pulled a face at him. "Well," she said, around another mouthful of toast and fig jam, "if it can be shown he died early in the afternoon, say shortly after lunch, Janet would have an alibi, whether it was natural causes or not."

But she knew enough from all she'd read, and all she'd learnt over the years, that pinpointing time of death was anything but an exact science. Especially when the timeframe was as small as a few hours, as it was in the case of Old Mr. Pickles.

Daniel shook his head. "But why did the old man leave the house to Janet? Had he argued with Charity and Nathaniel?"

"I have no idea. Last night was the first time I'd heard about it. It seems he'd only just told the family."

"So, you aren't intending to be involved in this while I'm here?"

"Not as far as I know," Emma assured him, fingers crossed. "Anyway, you'll be at the wharf all day today, seeing to the unloading, and the paperwork, and that repair, and whatever else needs doing. And tomorrow, you'll be spending the day with your son."

"Thank you for the list. I might have missed something if you hadn't reminded me." He grinned at her. The warm regard in his brown eyes, with just a hint of devilment, still had the power to lift her heart. "I'll just have to look forward to tomorrow then."

"Darcy certainly is," Emma said, knowing full well Daniel was too. And she had to give them time alone together. She didn't want them to grow apart. They'd have the weekend for the three of them. And the nights for just the two. Unfortunately, her pleasant thoughts on that were soured somewhat when Daniel urged her to steer clear of the Pickles' family problems.

He left, taking the *Mary B* the short distance to the wharf with the help of Abe, and crewman Blue Higgins, who had stayed on the boat as Daniel needed his help at the wharf.

Emma remained at the table enjoying another cup of tea, her notebook open in front of her. A timeline for where everyone was in the Pickles Boarding House on Wednesday afternoon could prove useful. Just in case. Getting it from the Pickles' ladies might be difficult, though. She couldn't see Charity being co-operative.

But it was a boarding house, after all, wasn't it? There could have been half a dozen guests in the house yesterday. Anyone could have killed Old Mr. Pickles. Emma brightened considerably at the thought.

"Janey, yesterday you mentioned the maid who works at the Pickles' Boarding House," she said, tapping her pencil.

Janey finished polishing the kettle and filled it with water. "You want me to go talk to her?"

It wasn't that easy, of course. A servant could get dismissed for revealing what they knew about their employer.

"Could you do it without Charity knowing?"

"You mean I can't just go knock on the door and invite myself in?" Janey said, eyes innocently wide.

"How would you react if someone knocked on our door and asked to speak to you about what goes on in this house?" Emma asked, eyeing her darkly.

Janey returned her look with a cheeky grin, and thoughtfully tapped her cheek with one finger. "Could be an interestin' chat."

Emma threw her pencil at the girl. Janey laughed as she caught it. Emma knew anyone asking such a question of her would get short shrift.

Janey twirled the pencil between her fingers. "The days I've seen Peggy it were Thursday, and she were doin' the shop with Miss Charity. Miss Charity," Janey repeated, emphasising the name, "takes lunch at the Tearoom and sends Peggy on errands. No nice lunch for her."

"You need to make a move, then," Emma said, getting to her feet. "You have to catch Peggy on her own today." She snatched the pencil from Janey's fingers.

"But what about my work? It don't get done by itself." Janey was now looking mutinous. "There's his clothes to be washed and ironed before Monday. And all the beddin', seein's how you won't send it to the laundry no more."

The bedding from the boat had become a contentious matter as Emma tried to rein in costs. It was hot, heavy work, boiling and stirring the sheets in the copper and putting them through the mangle. When she'd had Abe help Janey that one time they'd got into a right barney, and life had been unpleasant for days after.

"Alright, alright, we'll send the bedding to the laundry."

"Always and forever?"

Emma sighed but agreed. It was the sensible thing to do after all.

Janey picked up Emma's cup and saucer from the table where she'd left it.

"Oh, look, Miss Henrietta's comin' in," she said, catching movement out the window.

Chapter 6

Dr. MacArthur Makes a Judgement

EMMA OPENED the front door before Henrietta had a chance to knock.

"I have to be quick," Henrietta told her, barely pausing for breath. "I've left Janet on her own and I was hoping I might borrow Janey for an hour or so. Alice can't come in today and I need to see Dr. MacArthur."

"Are you unwell?" Emma asked. Henrietta did look flushed, but then she seemed to have been hurrying.

"No, no, it's about the autopsy."

"Have you heard the result already?" Emma found that surprising.

"No, oh, I'm not making myself clear, am I?"

"Not really. Come sit down for a moment. It will be quicker in the long run," Emma added, when Henrietta seemed about to protest, "and you obviously need to catch your breath. First things first. Janey," she said as they entered the kitchen, "you're needed at the Tearoom to give Janet a hand for a little while. You don't mind doing that do you?"

"Really?" Janey looked pleased. "Yeah, sure." Emma felt a frisson of concern. She hoped Janey wouldn't find working at the Primrose Tearoom more to her liking than working for her, even with no extra bedding to wash. "What about Peggy?" Janey asked.

"We'll talk about that later. You hurry along now and do whatever Janet needs you to."

"What was that about Peggy?" Henrietta asked when Janey had gone, and Emma had made them both a cup of tea. She seemed a little more relaxed now that Janet had some help.

"I thought Janey might be able to talk to Peggy and learn who was in the Pickles' house yesterday," Emma explained, "and what they were all doing. Just in case it was needed."

"Well, unless someone called in, there'd only be the four of them, Charity, Grace, Jonathon and Miriam. Nathaniel was at work."

"But what about the guests who are staying there?"

"Charity isn't having anyone to stay while Grace is visiting. She and Miriam are more work than the paying guests, according to her." So much for the idea of other suspects.

"And the autopsy?" she asked, as Henrietta gulped down a mouthful of tea, something she'd clearly been in need of.

Henrietta put a hand to her mouth for a moment. "I need to know what it shows, Emma," she said, worry etched between her eyes. "I told Janet it would be fine, but I don't like what that Sergeant said. Why shouldn't he arrest her, he said, when Miriam told him what she'd seen. I'm so messed up right now. I tried baking scones this morning and forgot the eggs."

"What is Nathaniel doing? Why doesn't he go and see about the autopsy?"

"Nat won't rock the boat," Henrietta said. Was there a tiny trace of bitterness there? "He'll wait until it becomes desperate before he'll act. And oftentimes it's too late then."

Emma hadn't seen that side of Nathaniel Pickles. She'd always thought him on top of things, certainly at the wharf anyway. Perhaps it was different when it was a personal matter.

"And Charity, or Grace?"

"Charity always left everything to her father, except for running the boarding house. I doubt she'll have any idea of what to do. Grace, I don't know, but she probably expects a man to deal with these things as well and isn't used to not having one around. Besides, it doesn't really matter to them, does it?"

Emma wasn't so sure about that. Her thoughts flew to the story she'd told Daniel that morning. She wanted to hear the results of the autopsy too. She knew Daniel wasn't going to like it when he heard what she'd done, but she said it anyway.

"Would you like me to come with you when you go to see Dr. MacArthur?"

"Would you?" Henrietta's look of relief, as she grabbed Emma's hand, sent Daniel's objections off in a puff of smoke.

THE DOCTOR'S ROOMS were modern, a two-storey brick construction built within the past few years on Heygarth Street. Emma wasn't sure who occupied the residence on the upper level, perhaps Doctor Rook, as she knew Dr. MacArthur had a smart residence on Percy Street. The area at the lower end of High Street was rapidly becoming the professional part of town. Across the street on the corner, was the town hall.

There were half a dozen patients in the waiting room when they entered. Emma had to force herself not to step back outside. The atmosphere was grey and depressing, and one elderly man was wheezing as if about to draw his last breath. She could only hope whatever was ailing him wasn't contagious.

She let Henrietta speak to the receptionist, asking for an interview with Dr. MacArthur or Dr. Rook regarding the death of her father-in-law. Speaking in hushed tones, the receptionist, a thin woman about Emma's age, her dark hair pulled back tightly into a low bun, informed them that Dr. MacArthur was performing the autopsy and should be free to speak to them in about half an hour. Would they care to take a seat and wait?

As they took the last two chairs in the room a door beside the receptionist's desk opened and a woman and child came out. Dr. Rook appeared, handing a folder to the receptionist, who handed him another one in return. He glanced at it.

"Miss Robinson," he said, and a woman in her twenties stood and followed him. As the door closed behind them, a collective sigh went round those waiting as they settled down to wait some more. The elderly man was still wheezing. Emma decided it sounded more like a miner's complaint than something contagious. Nothing you could do for that but alleviate the discomfort.

She opened her bag. She always carried a small supply of useful herbals, a lozenge or two of this and that she made for her family. Yes, there was one in the tin, a lozenge with echinacea and mint in the mixture. She must remember to make some more.

She stood and quietly approached the man. He looked at her in alarm as she held out the roughly shaped rectangular brown lozenge in her gloved fingers. She smiled.

"It will help," she said simply.

He took it and stared at it for moment, sniffed, shrugged, and put it in his mouth. What did he have to lose after all? Emma sat back down. Ten minutes later she looked up, startled. The elderly man stood before her. His colour had improved and his wheezing was less laboured.

"Do you have more of they?" he asked hopefully. Emma shook her head.

"Not with me, but I can make more," she hastened to tell him, as his expression drooped. "If you call in later next week. I live at the top of Watson Street. Ask for Mrs. Berry."

"Mrs. Berry, Watson Street," he muttered as he left the surgery. Several other patients were now looking at her with interest.

"You might have some more visitors than just him next week," Henrietta whispered. "Are you back in business?" Was that what she needed to be doing?

The receptionist was glaring at her, not pleased to see the back of a patient. She couldn't blame the woman. Here she was, seemingly peddling her wares in the doctors' very own business premises.

"I might be stepping on toes if I do," Emma whispered back.

"Perhaps you could supply the doctors," Henrietta suggested.

"Hmm, and have them charge twice the price." She'd think about it. A little extra money to cover the laundry costs wouldn't hurt either.

After another half hour, with patients coming and going, a light blinked on the receptionist's table. She left the waiting room to answer the summons. A few minutes later, the receptionist ushered Emma and

Henrietta into Dr. MacArthur's room, closing the door behind them as she left.

Dark wood paneling, shelves filled with leather bound books, and walls adorned with certificates and diplomas greeted them, oozing a refined and professional ambience intended, no doubt, to inspire a sense of authority. It immediately put Emma on edge. The man himself was seated behind a large, ornate desk, neat stacks of paper to one side, and a closed folder in front of him. He waved them toward two comfortable, upholstered chairs.

"Well, Mrs. Pickles, what is it you wish to know?" he asked, leaning back comfortably in his chair, his hands clasped loosely on his ample corporation.

"Can you tell us…" Henrietta's voice quavered for a moment, and Emma realised how anxious she must be feeling beneath her seemingly calm exterior. "I beg your pardon." She cleared her throat and tried again. "Can you please tell us how my father-in-law died?"

Dr. MacArthur leaned forward to flip open the folder. "I'm afraid, the indications are that he suffered a heart attack."

Henrietta's relief was palpable as her hand went to her chest. "Oh, thank goodness."

"Unfortunately, there is also the matter of the head wound," Dr MacArthur said, sitting back and thoughtfully stroking his dark whiskers with their hint of grey.

"The blow to the head was not in itself enough to cause death but the shock of it may have resulted in the heart attack which ultimately killed him."

"Oh. But…" Henrietta faltered.

"In which case," he went on, "the person who inflicted the head wound, in effect, killed him."

Henrietta looked about to faint. Emma reached out and squeezed her hand. "Doctor, what about time of death?" she asked. "There must be some indications as to when in the afternoon this heart attack occurred."

"Mrs. Berry. As you seem to have pointed out to my colleague, Doctor Rook, the room the deceased was found in was particularly warm. There had been very little cooling of the body when he made his preliminary examination."

Emma nodded. "That is perfectly true. Were the stomach contents examined? We know what time Mr. Pickles ate lunch. The degree of digestion could give us some indication of the time of death."

"And do you know what he ate for lunch?"

Emma realised she hadn't taken note of it herself. She looked to Henrietta, who was doing her best to hold up and follow the conversation.

"Tomato soup and a plain bread roll, no butter," she informed them.

"Oh." She should have asked Henrietta about that beforehand. Why couldn't Old Mr. Pickles have had a lamb chop, like any self-respecting male? The digestion of meat could be more readily measured. But tomato soup and a plain bread roll?

"Yes, not much help there I'm afraid," Dr. MacArthur said. Was he enjoying knocking down her suggestions? She had the distinct feeling he was.

"And lividity?" Emma felt she was clutching at straws.

"Again, no help, except to confirm he hadn't been moved. The time frame for his death is quite tight and not really in question, Mrs. Berry. It occurred within a period of little more than two hours, between when he returned from lunch, which is believed to have been somewhere between half past twelve and one o'clock, given when he left the place where he ate that meal, and when he was found dead at around three. It's not possible to tighten that time in any measurable way."

Emma frowned. She felt she was forgetting something.

"I'm not sure I understand what all that means," Henrietta spoke up. "If you can't say for certain when he died, how can you say it was the blow to the head that killed him. I mean, what if he was already dead and…"

"But why would someone hit him on the head if he was already dead?" Dr. MacArthur posed the question.

Henrietta shook her head, clearly bewildered.

"But he must have been," Emma spoke up again. "If his heart had still been pumping when the blow was landed there would have been a great deal of blood. Any wound to the head or face bleeds profusely, but there was virtually no blood at all. He must have been dead when he was struck."

"It is true that head wounds bleed a great deal. But what is to say the person who inflicted the blow didn't clean up the wound to give the illusion that death was by natural causes?"

Both Emma and Henrietta stared at the man. Was he acting as devil's advocate, or was he really trying to make a case for murder?

"Dr. MacArthur, a young woman has been accused of striking the blow, based on her having been found in the room with a piece of firewood in her hand. There is no sign of any clean up. No bloodied cloths, or bowls of water, or anything of that nature. It appears she had just that moment entered the room and found the firewood on the floor, as she claims."

"And well she could have, Mrs. Berry," Dr. MacArthur said reasonably. "The cleaning items could already have been disposed of. And then, realising she had left the incriminating log on the floor, she returns to the room intending to dispose of it in the fireplace and is, fortuitously, caught in the act."

"Or someone else had already delivered the blow and cleaned up, and she just happened to be the one who later found the piece of firewood on the floor,"

Emma said. "That is, after all, as acceptable an explanation as her returning to the room to dispose of it."

Dr. MacArthur's narrowed gaze and flared nostrils sent a shiver down Emma's spine. That she, a mere woman, should question his professional ability and suggest a competing interpretation of events. She felt suddenly ill. She was sure she'd just made the matter worse.

"Ladies," he said, his voice suave, "I appreciate your concerns, and it will of course be up to a court to decide the matter. But in my considerable experience the simple answer is usually the right one. I will, of course, be speaking to Sergeant Donovan who will no doubt be looking for the relevant evidence. Now, if you'll excuse me, I've given you as much time as I can."

Chapter 7

A Worrying Situation

HENRIETTA, distraught, grabbed Emma's arm as they stepped out onto the street.

"Oh, Emma. He's already condemned Janet. What are we going to do? This is dreadful. I can't believe..."

"Hush, hush," Emma soothed, urging the older woman along the street and away from the surgery windows. Despite trying to keep Henrietta calm, her own thoughts were running in an even wilder direction.

The story she'd related to Daniel just that morning came back to her with frightening clarity. Right now, she wanted to run and search the Pickles' washhouse for blood-stained cloths, in case they were later planted there. She took a shuddering breath and forced herself to speak calmly.

"We need to sit down, and have a cup of tea, and think this through," she said, for her own benefit as much as for Henrietta's.

Dr. MacArthur had said he'd be speaking to the Sergeant, who would in turn be looking for 'relevant evidence'. Emma interpreted that as meaning evidence to prove his theory, not evidence to point to the truth.

Henrietta, a handkerchief clutched in her hand to wipe away the tears, let Emma bear her away to the Tearoom. Lunch was underway when they arrived, and who should be enjoying it but Charity Pickles, sitting at a window table with Grace, Miriam, and Miriam's fiancé.

Henrietta took one look at them and turned away. Janey was clearing a table, but there was no sign of Janet. Emma followed Henrietta into the kitchen where they found Janet, skulking out of sight of the main room.

"I can't go out there," she said, looking wildly from one to the other. "Aunt Charity's been dreadful, giving me dirty looks and making comments among themselves. Several ladies left without ordering. I've had to let Janey look after the room. Did you find out anything? Please tell me you did."

Henrietta reached out and hugged her. "We need to talk about it."

"Oh, no. I'm going to be arrested, aren't I? But I didn't do anything."

"Hush, we'll sort it out." It was Henrietta's turn to calm.

Janey came in balancing a tray piled high with dirty plates and cutlery which she took into the scullery.

"We need to close for a few hours," Henrietta decided. "I can't bear to talk to anyone right now. Who else is out there?" she asked, as Janey returned to the kitchen.

"There's just the two tables finishing off their teapot," she reported. "And Miss Charity's lot."

"Why don't you two go into the house," Emma told Henrietta and Janet. "Janey and I will see them off and lock up, and then we'll come and join you." The sound of clinking crockery sounded from the scullery. "Is someone else here?"

"Only Peggy," Janey replied.

Emma stared at her. "Peggy? The Pickle's maid, Peggy?"

"You wanted me to talk to her," Janey said, arcing up as usual at the idea she was being questioned about her behaviour.

"Janey, you're brilliant. I have a job for the two of you." She turned to Henrietta and Janet. "But we'll need to keep Charity and the rest of them here for as long as we can. Quickly now. We can't waste this opportunity."

Ten minutes later Emma came out of the kitchen with a tray holding a fresh pot of tea, a plate of jam and cream scones, and two extra cups, all of which she placed on Charity's table. She was followed by Henrietta.

"I need to apologise," Henrietta told them, as she and Emma pulled up two extra chairs to the end of the table.

"Apologise?" Charity said, with a hard edge of disbelief. Henrietta picked up the teapot and topped up everyone's cup.

"Yes. With the stress of what was happening yesterday I didn't get the opportunity to introduce you all properly. I know you've met Emma, Charity, but the rest of the family haven't. Do help yourself to the scones," Henrietta said, pushing the plate forward. With that, she formally introduced Emma to Charity's sister, Grace Hewitt, Grace's daughter Miriam, and Miriam's fiancé, Jonathan Inglis. The usual pleasantries were exchanged, albeit a little strained.

"Are you planning on staying long in Echuca?" Emma asked Grace politely, doing her best to pretend this was a pleasant social interaction, and that she and Henrietta hadn't just hijacked the table. Looks were exchanged between the family members.

"Well, until this matter of the house is decided, at least," Grace replied hesitantly.

"Ah, do you have something to offer on that subject?" Charity cut in. "Is that what this tea party is about? Janet will let us have the house if we don't have her charged with murder? Is that it?"

Henrietta looked as if she were about to faint. Emma was afraid Charity might drag the family away at any moment. She had to give her a reason to stay.

"We spoke to Dr. MacArthur, the Coroner, this morning, Miss Pickles," she said. "Henrietta thought the sooner we all knew what had happened the better, before more accusations were thrown about and a real rift created in the family. According to the autopsy, your father died of a heart attack."

"Well, at least we don't have a murderer in the family," Charity said, "even if it doesn't change the outcome."

"But he was hit on the head," Miriam exclaimed. "The doctor said so. He saw the wound."

"That's true," Emma said. She hesitated. How did she tell them about Dr. Macarthur's conclusion?

"But could it have caused the heart attack?" Jonathan Inglis spoke up for the first time, saving her the trouble to explain. Unfortunately, it also meant another one who might accept that theory.

"Yes, that must be what happened," Miriam agreed. "I'm truly sorry, Aunt Henrietta, but I can only tell the police what I saw."

"Of course," Henrietta all but whispered. Emma knew she wanted to go hide in the kitchen but hoped her friend could hang on a little longer.

"So that must mean Janet killed him," Charity said. "If she caused his heart attack."

Miriam nodded. "That's right."

"An event such as that would have been a great shock to an elderly and frail man," Jonathon commented.

"Is that what Dr. MacArthur believes happened?" Charity asked.

"It would appear so," Emma found herself having to acknowledge. Regardless of how unpleasant Charity Pickles might be, she wasn't stupid. Emma imagined they would all be happy to see Janet removed from the equation so they could claim their inheritance. Except perhaps Nathaniel. But as a man, he was able to earn a living out in the world, so the inheritance wasn't of such vital importance to him, and Janet was his daughter, after all.

"I don't believe Janet would throw us out of the house, anyway," Grace said, seemingly more concerned about her future than with what Janet might have done.

"Well, I'm not running that place just for her to prosper," Charity told them.

"She'd have to pay you, Charity," Grace responded. "You can't tell me Father had you doing all that work for nothing."

"You won't be getting free board and lodging, either," Charity shot back at her. "Don't think that for a moment."

"I don't understand why Father would have done this. You and Nathaniel must have made him terribly angry about something," Grace accused.

"We didn't do anything. It was that niece of ours, working behind our backs, undermining us, the little worm."

"Janet knew nothing about this, Charity," Henrietta cried. "Don't you dare accuse her of such a thing."

"But she killed him," Miriam argued. "He must have been going to change his will back again. That's why she did it. She'll go to prison now. She has to."

"Will she, Jonathon? Will there be a trial?" Grace asked.

Jonathon Inglis looked reluctant to comment. Given the acrimony at the table Emma wasn't surprised if he wanted to remain at arm's length. "Well, there's the wound to the head. Someone was seen with a piece of firewood in their hand at the scene, which was apparently thrown into the fireplace and burnt. Then there's an argument over an inheritance, so a possible motive." He nodded. "A case could be made."

"Are you involved with the law, Mr. Inglis?" Emma asked. That analysis hadn't come from a layman, she didn't think.

"I am a barrister, recently admitted to the bar," he said, smiling.

"He's brilliant," Miriam asserted.

"Perhaps you should engage Mr. Inglis to defend Janet, Henrietta," Charity said drily.

"I'd be happy to do it," Jonathan said, earning a glare from Charity, who clearly was being facetious with her suggestion. "Though I hope it won't come to that," he added hastily. "But I would do it pro bono, as it's family. Please don't hesitate if it becomes necessary, Mrs. Pickles. You would only need to put me in touch with your attorney."

"Thank you," Henrietta said faintly.

Charity pulled on her gloves. "Well, this is all very interesting, but we really must be getting on. I don't know where the time is going to these days."

Henrietta and Emma exchanged a look of alarm. Had they given Janey and Peggy enough time?

"I hope you enjoyed your lunch," Henrietta said to Grace.

"Lunch was quite delicious," Grace replied, as she gathered up her bag and gloves. "You have a lovely little place here."

"You must come by again while you're in town," Henrietta urged. "And if there's anything you'd really enjoy I'd be only too pleased to serve it to you."

"That's very thoughtful of you. I will keep it in mind."

Henrietta took her time unlocking the front door. Jonathan Inglis held the door open as she followed the other family members out to the street for a last goodbye.

"It was very kind of you to offer your professional services for Janet, Mr. Inglis," Emma said, doing her best to delay their departure further. "But tell me, in your opinion, do you believe you will be needed?"

"Oh, I'm quite sure..." he began. Emma was certain he was about to politely brush off her concerns, but as his dark blue eyes met her own green ones, he seemed to check for a moment. "The situation does concern me, Mrs. Berry," he finished.

Emma nodded. "I appreciate your honesty, Mr. Inglis." Worrying as it was.

He inclined his head to her and joined the ladies. Henrietta stared after them as they moved off down the street, before popping back into the cafe, a look of relief on her face.

"Janey's just turned in between the buildings," she reported breathlessly. "I didn't see Peggy."

"Thank goodness." There was no way Emma would've been able to explain it away if Janey had been caught at the boarding house. "Let's hear what she has to say."

Henrietta locked the door. "I don't want to be nice to people right now," she said, when Emma sent her a questioning glance.

Janey was already placing the kettle over the fire when Emma and Henrietta joined her in the kitchen.

"Did you find anything?" Emma asked at once and was immediately relieved when Janey shook her head.

"No buckets of bloodied water, or bloodied washcloths," she reported, seeming to savour the words. She selected a clean teapot from the shelf above the bench. "And nothing out of place Peggy could tell."

"Good, well done. So, if something turns up that suggests a cleanup, we'll know it's been planted," Emma said.

"You don't really think the police would do such a thing, do you?" Henrietta asked.

"I hope not, but best to be a step ahead, just in case." It wasn't only the police she was suspicious of, after all. Whoever hit Old Mr. Pickles on the head could take it into their own head to concoct more evidence against Janet too. She wasn't going to pass that thought on to Henrietta though.

Janey put tea leaves in the teapot as the kettle began to sing.

"What did you do with Peggy?" Emma asked.

"Left her peeling potatoes for dinner."

"Charity will be pleased to see that, anyway," Henrietta said with a laugh.

"She won't ever say so," Janey commented.

"No."

Janet came in through the back door. "Who won't ever say so?" she asked.

"Your Aunt Charity. She won't ever compliment a maid on something well done," Henrietta told her daughter.

Janet laughed without humour. Having worked at the boarding house in years past, she knew her aunt's personality very well. "I saw Aunt Charity's lot leave from upstairs," she said now. "How did it go?"

"Charity and Grace were at one another's throats the whole time, but nothing unusual in that," Henrietta told her. "But Jonathan offered to defend you if it came to a trial. Free of charge, too."

Janet's expression froze. Emma thought her friend wasn't sure if the offer was a blessing or not. To have a defence free of cost, yes, but the necessity of it, no.

"Well, that's awfully good of him," she managed to say. "How did Miriam take his offer?"

"I didn't notice."

"I thought her smile seemed a bit fixed," Emma said, as Henrietta looked to her. "I get the feeling she isn't as sure of him as she'd like to be."

"That's not what Peggy says," Janey told her.

"And what does Peggy say?"

"She doesn't like that Miriam. Says she's full of herself and orders her man about."

Emma tried not to smile. It was Miriam that Janey was describing and not herself, wasn't it? But people's relationships and perceptions were interesting. Perhaps what Peggy saw was a confident woman telling her man what to do, when Miriam's reality was about getting reassurance that he cared enough to do as she wanted.

Chapter 8

Another Possible Suspect

JANET GATHERED up cups and saucers and took them to the table in the middle of the kitchen, while Henrietta went into the cafe and returned with the plate of scones that had barely been touched. Janey carried the teapot to the table and began to pour as they all sat.

"How did Peggy come to be here in the Tearoom, anyway?" Emma asked, helping herself to a scone.

"She had bags of shopping to take home when Miss Charity and the rest came in for lunch, and Sonny was hanging about outside," Janey said, referring to a coloured man about Emma's age who ran messages and did odd jobs for whoever wanted to hire him, when he was around, "so I got 'im to help her with the bags, and for both of 'em to come back for a bit of lunch."

"That was very enterprising of you," Emma encouraged. Janey gave her a sideways look as if unsure whether she was being praised or not. "Well done," Emma added for good measure. "But did she tell you anything about yesterday?"

Janey swallowed a mouthful of scone. "I didn't have time to talk to her at lunch time. We were busy cooking, and then I had to be out serving and cleaning up the tables, and Peggy was doing the dishes, and then you came."

Well, it was a bit much to expect, but at least Janey had made a connection with the girl. She'd have to think about how to make use of that later.

"Oh, and guess what, Mum," Janet said, "Sonny fixed that dripping tap in the washroom while he was here."

"And what did that cost? I thought Alex was going to do it."

"Alex hasn't time to do all the odd jobs around here, Mum, and Sonny did it in return for lunch," Janet told her with a touch of asperity. "He was really sorry to hear about Grandfather. I don't think he has had much work for Sonny lately, though." Her shoulders slumped. "I just wish I'd been able to talk to him yesterday when he was here for lunch, but we couldn't very well talk about it in public, could we?" Everyone agreed that that wouldn't have worked. "So, I was really pleased when I got his note asking me to call. I know he could be difficult to get along with," she said sadly, "but I didn't want to be arguing with him. I was just hoping we could sort out this business of me inheriting the boarding house."

"He wasn't an easy man to get on with," Henrietta said. "He never said much, and he had definite ideas, which it was almost impossible to change. And pernickety, as Charity said. But of all things, he was a gentleman."

"He was," Janet agreed. Emma had the impression that both women had cared for Old Mr. Pickles, despite his idiosyncrasies.

Emma topped up her cup. "You'd only recently learnt he was leaving the boarding house to you, I believe," she said, remembering the accusations hurled around in the Pickles' parlour the previous evening.

Janet rubbed her forehead. "The first we all knew about it was over dinner on Monday. Aunt Grace had arrived the day before and we were all there for dinner. Just as we'd finished dessert, Grandfather said this was a good time to tell us about his will, and that he was leaving his estate to me."

"That must have come as a shock to all of you."

"Did it ever. I mean ... Dad and my aunts were expecting to get it all. They've believed that forever, haven't they, Mum?"

"That's always been my understanding."

"I thought Aunt Charity was going to leap over the table and strangle me on the spot. Aunt Grace looked about to faint, and even Dad didn't look too well pleased. I told Grandfather I didn't want the house. I had all I needed. But he said it wasn't open to discussion."

Emma frowned. "And you had no idea of this?"

"Absolutely none. Like I said, I tried later to speak to him, but he wouldn't talk about it. I was feeling more than a bit desperate. This was going to break the family apart and create all sorts of problems, but I had no idea how I would change his mind, so when I got his note yesterday, I thought Aunt Grace might have convinced him to change his will. Or perhaps have him put in something about them being able to live there for as long as they wanted. Miriam wouldn't need a home there because she was going to marry Jonathon."

"Did he expect you would move into the house," Emma asked, "and have your father and aunts move out?" It did seem an outrageous idea.

Henrietta certainly thought so. "As if she would do a thing like that," she said, indignant.

"I don't know what he expected, Emma," Janet said, clearly frustrated and upset. "He just said it was for the best. Now, I'm not sure what to do. I'd like to just give the house back to Dad and my aunts, but then I feel I'm going against what Grandfather wanted. I wish I understood why he left it to me rather than his children. He just never explained it."

"It's alright, love," Henrietta said patting her daughter's hand. But it wasn't, and they all knew it.

"What do you think really happened yesterday?" She asked Emma.

"Well, it doesn't make sense that Charity, Grace, or Nathaniel would kill their father over the will. They would have talked to him, tried to convince him to change it. But then…if he refused, as it seems he would, one of them might have hit him out of frustration and anger. Perhaps Nathaniel slipped away from his office and…"

"No." Henrietta and Janet both said at once.

"Never. Nat would never consider such a thing," Henrietta added.

"No," Janet repeated shaking her head. "That can be easily proved, anyway, if he never left the wharf."

That was true enough. She might be able to get Daniel to make discreet enquiries about that. It could be easily proved, as Janet said. One way or the other.

"Was Miriam in the parlour when you went in?" she asked Janet, realising she didn't have a clear picture of how it had gone down.

"No, she came in almost right away, though. I let myself in as usual, and I knew he'd be in the parlour. He always was these days. I thought he was asleep. It was Miriam who looked at him properly, when he didn't wake when she spoke to him."

"And the firewood?"

"It was lying beside his chair, as if he'd dropped it, so I just picked it up and was about to put it in the basket when she came in." She frowned and acted out a movement with her hand. "I did put it in the basket," she said. "It was empty, and I dropped it in as she was speaking to him."

"Did she accuse you of killing him then?"

"Not right away. She spoke to him, and when he didn't answer she looked more closely. She screamed then." Emma wasn't surprised, seeing him staring with unseeing eyes. It had set her back a little, too. "Jonathan, and then Aunt Charity and Aunt Grace came rushing in, and Peggy was sent to get Dad, and then Mum came, and then you did."

"So, when did Miriam start accusing you of killing your grandfather?"

"When Dad noticed the wound on his head. She said she knew something wasn't right when she came in and saw me standing beside Grandfather with the firewood in my hand."

This wasn't good. They needed other suspects. Who would believe Janet didn't want the Pickles' house, regardless of what she might claim? Or that she hadn't killed her grandfather when he threatened to disinherit her? Emma just didn't know how, with no other suspects, they could prove she didn't do it.

"Peggy says he was arguing with someone when he come back from lunch," Janey announced.

"What?" Emma knew she was staring open-mouthed at the girl. "You said you hadn't talked to her."

"I said I didn't get to talk to her at lunch time. We talked when you sent us to check if there'd been a cleanup."

"Oh, my stars. Someone else was in the house?"

"Who? Who was it?" Henrietta asked, equally eager to know.

"Peggy didn't see him. She heard the old man come in with someone and they was arguing. They went into the parlour."

"Where was she when she heard them, then, if she didn't see him?" Emma asked.

"She was in the dining room. Miss Charity had sent her to change the tablecloth and throw out the flowers."

"I don't suppose Peggy heard what they were saying, Janey?"

"She heard the other man say, "You're being unreasonable," and then the door to the parlour closed, and she could only hear their voices."

"Was he there for long?"

Janey shook her head. "She was upstairs after that. She might have heard a door slam later, but she wasn't sure."

"I wonder if anyone else in the house heard anything." Something else to ask the Pickles sisters. Was this the answer they needed?

"Could it have been Mr. Collins?" Janet said now, her face alight. "He was talking to Grandfather outside the Tearoom, wasn't he?"

"Yes, of course," Emma said. "And Janey and I saw them walk off down the street together. How well do they know one another?" Though she thought they must have known one another quite well when she considered what she'd seen in that brief moment outside the Tearoom.

"They have some business together," Henrietta said. "Nathaniel would know more about it. Does this mean there really could be someone else who hit him, the poor man," she said hope flaring.

"Well, yes, whoever it turns out to be, if it wasn't Henry Collins. It gives us someone else with an opportunity. Oh, my. I should have thought of Henry Collins. It just didn't occur to me that he might have been in the house."

There was the sound of someone trying to open the front door to the Tearoom.

"Oh, look at the time. We need to open up again," Henrietta said, pushing her chair back. "They'll be knocking the door down for their afternoon teas any minute. Are you going to be all right to keep working, Janet?"

"I guess so. At least Aunt Charity's not likely to be back today." Everyone seemed to have had a resurgence of energy at the idea of a possible new suspect.

Emma hesitated for just a moment. "Would you like Janey to stay a while longer?"

"Would you?" Janet asked her. "We need to bake, and Peggy didn't get to finish the washing up."

"How come she was doing it anyway?" Henrietta asked, turning back for moment.

"She's putting her trousseau together, so I offered her a sixpence for helping," Janet explained. "She was awfully grateful."

Henrietta shook her head. "Sixpences have a habit of adding up," she said, and went to unlock the front door.

"And we only have one pair of hands each," Janet said, refusing to be chastised. She looked at the empty plate in front of them that had once held a goodly number of scones.

"Come on then, Janey. A pot of tea to keep them quiet, and then we have to bake scones, biscuits and a twenty-minute cake."

EMMA COLLECTED Darcy from school on the way home from the Tearoom.

"Is Dad at home?" was the first thing he said to her.

"Oh, don't I even get a hello?" Emma gently scolded.

"Sorry. Hello, Mummy. Is Dad at home?"

"That's a little bit better, anyway. But the answer is, I don't know. I haven't been home since this morning."

"He told me he was going to the wharf today. Can we go to the wharf, Mummy, please?"

"But he might be at home already."

"Ple-e-ase."

"Alright, don't whine. But we'll go home first because it's closer, and if he's not there, we can go to the wharf after you've changed out of your uniform."

"Yes!"

Darcy raced ahead. When Emma, walking quickly, rounded the corner into their short strip of Watson Street, Darcy was leaning impatiently on their locked front door.

"Looks like Dad's not home then," she said as she fished in her bag for her keys.

Ten minutes later they were on their way to the wharf, Darcy in knickerbockers and a flat cap. Emma insisted that he walk like the young gentleman he was, thankful that none of his teachers had seen him running like a street urchin earlier. At least she hoped they hadn't, but a boy had to run sometimes.

Down the length of Watson Street they walked, past Hopwood Square where the carts, wagons and sheep used to gather to cross the river to New South Wales on Hopwood's ferry. Now there was an iron bridge across the Murray at the far end of town and the Square was just sand, gravel and weeds.

Past the Square, the river was lined with riverboats and barges. Some boats had people living permanently on board, moving location occasionally as the whim took them, others stood empty. Closer to the wharf were those waiting for their next load, or with cargo and wool to unload.

The wharf itself was busy with cranes clanking and whirring, and men in and out of the cargo shed where the office was also located. Emma's heart beat faster as she felt the wharf timbers beneath her feet. She missed being part of this. But times were changing.

Echuca was losing out on the transport of goods downriver. The cost of getting goods up by train the hundred and thirty miles from Melbourne, couldn't compete with the same items coming from Adelaide at the far end of the Murray, which was much closer to its main river port at Goolwa. To Emma, it was just another reason for Darcy to need other options for his future.

"There he is," Darcy cried now, pointing to the *Mary B*'s distinctive yellow and black striped funnel showing above the wharf at the far end. It was billowing steam.

Chapter 9

What To Do Next

"QUICK, WE MIGHT get a ride," Emma urged, not that Darcy needed any encouragement as, holding his hand tightly to keep him from getting in the way, they half ran, half walked, keeping as close as possible to the shed. At the far end of the wharf, a crane was moving wool bales from a barge to the rail cars waiting on the spur line for transport to Melbourne.

They took to the steps that led down to the narrow lower walkway, which Emma saw was almost at water level. Her hopes rose that the river levels might hold for a few more months, and they could travel downriver to Wirramilla for Christmas this year.

She could see Daniel in the cockpit. He couldn't help but notice them as they came abreast. She couldn't see Abe, but Blue Higgins was further down the walkway, about to untie the mooring ropes. He grinned at Emma and leapt onto the boat, his long, lanky frame making it look easy, before loping along to the cockpit.

"Passengers comin' aboard, Capt'n."

"Yeah, okay Blue. I see them."

Blue put down the boarding plank and handed Emma and Darcy on board. They joined Daniel in the cockpit, as Blue took up the boarding plank before hopping back onto the walkway to release the ropes.

"See you bright and early Monday," Daniel called to him. Blue waved them off and Daniel eased the boat away from the wharf.

"Thought we might take a little trip upriver on Sunday, if the weather's fine," Daniel said, "find a nice spot for a picnic." He looked over Darcy's head and met Emma's smiling gaze. "Would you like that?"

"Sounds wonderful."

"Can Jemmy come?" Darcy asked.

"Don't see why not," Daniel told him.

He steered the *Mary B* into the centre of the river and turned her, heading to the far end of Watson Street, where he circled again to bring her against the bank below their house, facing back upriver. Daniel rang down to the engine room and Emma heard the whistle of the steam as the pressure was released from the boiler and felt the *Mary B* settle.

As they stepped out of the cockpit and made their way down the stairs to the lower deck, Abe appeared from the engine room.

"Make sure you douse the fire," Daniel told him.

"I done it." Daniel nodded. Abe put down the boarding plank and waited as they all crossed to the riverbank.

Over the years, Daniel had terraced the bank, piling the dirt removed up at the top as a barrier to flooding, and creating several flat terraces that also acted as stairs, when the river wasn't running high. It made the riverbank safer for Darcy and his friends, and Emma loved what he'd done.

She enjoyed sitting out on the terraces on summer evenings, with folding chairs, a glass of wine and some food, or just lazing on a blanket under the stars, the water lapping below. Having the *Mary B* there now created a glow in her heart. Life would be perfect at this moment, she thought, if it weren't for a death weighing on her mind.

Darcy's friend, Jemmy, was waiting for them on the verandah as they made their way up the bank, his eyes huge as he gazed down at the *Mary B*.

"Can we go on it?"

"Yeah," Darcy said, all casual.

"No," Daniel said. "The boiler's still hot, and I don't want you messing about in the cockpit."

"I could keep an eye on 'em," Abe offered.

"Go on," Emma encouraged. "I'm sure you could do with a quiet cup of tea right now."

"Oh, fair enough. You two make sure you do as Abe tells you, though, or I'll tan your hides, both of you." The boys didn't need telling twice as they joined Abe on the boat.

In the kitchen, Janey had left the fire in the cooker banked and, with the help of some kindling, Emma managed to get it burning brightly again.

"Where's Janey?" Daniel wanted to know. Tea was going to be some time in coming.

"She's helping at the Tearoom. I'm just hoping she doesn't enjoy it too much and decide to take it on permanently."

Daniel laughed as he took a seat in the dining nook. "I wouldn't worry. They both get far more freedom working here. They're part of the family, anyway. Abe will be as happy as the boys messing about on the boat."

"I'm glad you feel that way." He'd always seemed to resent what he called her easy life, with servants, but he'd clearly found over the years that it made life more pleasant. And she'd not only grown up with Janey, but Janey was also Nella's half-sister, having the same mother, and Nella was in turn Emma's half-sister, having the same father.

She had a sudden yearning to see Nella and Lucy, and her parents. Especially her parents. Their continuing existence felt more tenuous since her grandmother had died.

"Do you think we might be able to spend Christmas at Wirramilla this year? I'd really like to."

"It depends on the water levels, Em, you know that." The river had been a series of pools by early December for the past two years. Trade and travel had been severely restricted as drought hit the country.

"We could take the coach."

Daniel grimaced, as she knew he would. She'd drop the matter for now. She'd put the idea in his head, so she'd just have to wait it out. But then an even better idea popped into her head.

Why couldn't they spend the whole off-season at Wirramilla for a change? Arrive on the last of the water and leave when it was high enough again in the new year. Daniel would have plenty to occupy himself between the *Mary B* and life on the station. He got on well with Joe too, and he and Catherine were sure to visit from Wentworth with their two children. Darcy would love spending time with his cousins.

"How was your day?" Daniel asked now, bringing her back to reality but leaving the idea simmering in the back of her mind. "Anything new on the Pickles matter?"

"Quite a lot," Emma said. She cut some slices from a fruit cake as the kettle started to sing. "Did you get everything done that you needed today?"

"I did. I pick up the cargo first thing Monday."

"Good, then you'll be free to spend tomorrow with Darcy." It also meant she would be free to deal with Old Mr. Pickles death.

She made the tea and sat to tell him about Dr. Mac-Arthur's conclusion from the autopsy, speaking to Charity, and the possibility of a suspect that wasn't a member of the Pickles family. She left out Janey and Peggy's search at the Pickles' house. He certainly wouldn't approve of that.

"I was hoping you could check up on Nathaniel Pickles' movements at some time," she said. "Discreetly, of course," she added as Daniel looked at her sharply. Henrietta and Janet didn't believe he would have killed his father, but Emma thought he might have argued with him about the will and lost his temper when the old man remained stubborn.

"It isn't any of your business, Emma. That's what we have the police for. I'd really prefer you keep out of it, especially as it seems to be getting nasty."

"My friends have asked for my help," Emma replied, hoping Daniel wouldn't forbid her to be involved. She wasn't sure she'd be able to comply, and they'd end up at an impasse. She reached for his hand. "I really need to do this."

"Is life a bit dull for you now?"

Oh, was he going to suggest she should move back onto the *Mary B*? Were they going to have another argument about Darcy's schooling? When she first broached her ideas on that subject, it had been almost as bad as George MacDonald not allowing Bea to go to Miss Marshall's School for Young Ladies all those years ago. Except she'd had no say in that.

"No, of course it isn't," she insisted, girding up for an argument.

Daniel opened his mouth to say more but she was saved from hearing it as Janey came in at the front door at that moment, just as Ah Sing sang out a greeting from the back verandah. Daniel huffed in frustration. Perhaps having servants in the house didn't always please him if it meant not being able to speak when he wanted.

"It's definitely never dull around here," Emma insisted, and joined Janey, who had gone straight on down the hall to meet Ah Sing, the Chinese vegetable gardener. Ah Lo was with him, and Ah Sing was holding a scaled and gutted Murray Cod. Emma had forgotten she'd spoken to him about fishing and the possibility of his catching one for her. Another lapse of memory. Was she in need of a herbal remedy for herself?

Emma sent Janey to fetch her purse so she could pay for the fish while she chatted to the two Chinese men. Daniel came out and greeted them, and Emma hoped that would be the end of any contentious conversations tonight.

Emma slept badly, her mind wandering over just how she was to go about her questioning of the Pickles family for a timeline of what everyone had been doing on Wednesday. It went without saying that no family with any self-respect wanted a murderer among their number. If they were outraged at the idea, or afraid, they might start giving out some useful information, perhaps hinting at another family member.

She wouldn't repeat her request to Daniel to check on Nathaniel Pickles' movements. She'd do that herself. She'd need to step delicately though.

And then there was Henry Collins. Should she start with him tomorrow? She might be able to solve the matter quickly, supposing he was the guilty one. Supposing he would even deign to speak to her, of course.

But what was his motive? He'd argued with Old Mr. Pickles, according to the maid, Peggy, but about what? How acrimonious had it been, and what was at stake? She had no idea.

When she finally fell asleep, the only conclusion she'd reached was that, while she didn't know enough about Henry Collins to conduct a useful interview, that very lack of knowledge would provide a perfect excuse for talking to Nathaniel Pickles, who would know.

"What are you and Darcy planning on doing today?" Emma asked Daniel over breakfast next morning, stifling a yawn.

"Thought we might wander downriver a way and try a spot of fishing." Emma wondered if Ah Sing's visit had put the idea in his head. "And I haven't seen old Fred for some time. Might call in there later. He'd like to see Darcy too, I'm sure."

"Remember me to him," Emma told Daniel. Fred Croaker had been the best crewman any riverboat ever had as far as she was concerned, and a great friend to her when they'd travelled together. His health wasn't the best these days. Only Blue Higgins and Ah Lo remained of the *Mary B*'s old crew now. Both Willy Bowman and Shorty Mason had moved on. She'd completely lost trace of them.

She saw Henrietta hurry past on her way to the Tearoom from her house next door and wondered how she was holding up.

Once breakfast was over, Daniel and Darcy went down to the garden shed to sort out their fishing gear. Emma waited for them to leave before beginning her own day.

"Are we going out?" Janey asked, as Emma came into the kitchen with her bag, and her hat and gloves on.

"I am. I'm not sure if I'll be home for lunch so you just look after yourself and Abe."

"Won't you need some help talking to people?"

"Not today, Janey, but I am following up on what you learnt from Peggy yesterday." Emma hesitated for a moment. "Did you enjoy working at the Tearoom?"

"It was alright." Janey flicked an imaginary crumb off the table.

"Just alright?"

"In the kitchen was good. Janet, Mrs. Naughton, is real nice. But I didn't like bein' in the cafe."

"Were people rude to you?"

"Some of them looked at me odd like."

Emma thought Janey should probably be used to that, as people could be wary of those with darker skin. Coloured servants usually kept to the background, so seeing one front and centre in the Tearoom may have upset the sensibilities of some customers.

"If Henrietta or Janet need help next time, perhaps we could say you're only to work in the kitchen." She didn't think it right, but she didn't want Janey to feel uncomfortable either.

Janey gave a half shrug. "I guess. They look at me like that when I have lunch there with you, too. Peggy thinks I'm being bold and getting above myself."

"I'm sorry to hear that. But seriously, Janey, it doesn't matter what other people think. You just need to be yourself." Not that Emma thought Janey had any trouble holding her own. "Peggy's probably a little jealous that you get to have lunch at the Tearoom," she added.

Janey grinned at that. "Oh yeah. She doesn't get any of that. She doesn't like them Pickles ladies much. It's all, do this, do that. And they're nothing special, she says. Miss Grace is short of money, and she and

Miss Charity snipe all the time and it made the old man angry."

Well, the animosity between the sisters wasn't anything new, and Emma had already gathered that Grace's future wasn't looking overly bright, but it was useful to have that confirmed. At least it didn't seem she was about to lose Janey to the Tearoom any time soon, which was a relief.

"You know you can invite Peggy here for afternoon tea anytime if you'd like. If you're going to be friendly with her."

"Might do that sometime."

Abe came in from the yard. "I've got the fire started..." He stared at her, dressed to go out. "Didn't you say we were makin' that liniment today?"

Emma's hand went to her mouth. "Oh, Abe, I'm sorry. I completely forgot. It will have to wait, I'm afraid. I can't possibly do it right now."

Abe shrugged. "You're the boss."

"Everythin' gets put aside when she's huntin' a killer," Emma heard Janey tell him, as she shut the front door.

Chapter 10

Where is Everyone?

EMMA TOOK HERSELF along Watson Street again in the direction of the wharf. Only one crane was working this morning, loading the PS *Warren* and its barge with goods from the shed. She slipped into the office, located to the side of the shed entrance, and nodded at several of the riverboat captains she knew who doffed their caps to her.

She was surprised not to see Nathaniel Pickles at his usual high desk behind the counter, overseeing everything that went on.

"Is Mr. Pickles around somewhere?" she asked Mr. Norman, his offsider.

Mr. Norman peered at her over his half-spectacles, the skin around his grey eyes crinkling as he offered her a rather sad smile.

"He was called away a little time ago, Mrs. Berry. Mrs. Pickles called for him. Right upset she was too."

"Henrietta?" He nodded. "Do you know what it was about?"

"She didn't say, not in my hearing, anyway. Something to do with the father's death I shouldn't wonder."

Emma thanked him and took a direct path behind the wharf to High Street, making her way between the salt works shed and the Bridge Hotel. She had to wait a moment for several wagons to pass before crossing to the Tearoom. She knew the door would be locked before she'd even tried it. The blinds were drawn on both the glass door and the windows.

Down the side of the building, she hurried to the front door of Janet's house, but there was no answer to her knock. Not even the nanny and the children were at home. What was going on? The Pickles' house was the obvious next stop, and only two streets away.

Peggy opened the door to her knock. Her eyes widened in alarm, her hand going to her mouth when she saw who it was, as if Emma were about to report what she and Janey had gotten up to the day before.

Emma put a finger to her lips and shook her head. "Could I speak to Mr. Nathaniel Pickles please?" she said.

"Um, he's at work," Peggy said.

"Who is it?" Charity wanted to know, stepping out of the parlour, and grimacing when she saw Emma.

"I'm looking for your brother," Emma told her. "Apparently, Henrietta called him away from work, but the Tearoom is closed and there's no one home at Janet's house."

"Nathaniel went off to work as usual this morning," Charity said, as Grace appeared behind her. "And the Tearoom's closed?" She sniffed. "Perhaps they've taken Janet and all skipped town. Can't say I'm surprised."

"But they can't do that," Grace cried. "They'll need money to live on. They'll have to sell the house. What are we going to do?"

"Why are you asking me?" Charity snapped. "Your husband should have provided for you." Emma couldn't entirely blame Charity for her ill humour. Losing her father, and now her home was enough to make anyone sour at the world, and Charity Pickles hadn't had far to go on that score.

But she didn't want to get caught up in the Pickles sisters' drama. "I'll keep looking for them," she said, and saw herself out as voices rose in acrimony behind her.

But Janet's family skipping town? Emma couldn't see it, but she was getting a very bad feeling about what might be going on. Should she go to the police station? But if they had left town, she'd be drawing police attention to them. She'd try the livery stable first. Alex, Janet's husband, would know if something was happening with his wife, though if the whole family had disappeared, he and the children would be with them. At least that might confirm the situation.

Emma hurried back up High Street, turning left past the Town Hall into Heygarth, and then right into

Hare Street. She stopped and waited as a lady and gentleman trotted out of the livery stable premises on their smart horses, looking to be going for a pleasant ride in the country. It had been a long time since she'd been riding.

In the little lean-to off the stable itself she looked for Alex. Not finding him, or anyone else there, she ventured into the stable.

"Is Alex around," she asked a lad who was backing a horse into the shafts of a chaise.

"He's been called away."

"I don't suppose you know why, or where to?"

The lad pulled a note from his vest pocket and handed it to her. "He dropped this and lit out like his pa… fast like."

Emma opened the note. The handwriting was shaky, much the way she felt as she stared at it.

Janet's been arrested.

She scrunched the note in her hand and hurried away without another word, retracing her steps up High Street. Anyone seeing her dashing back and forth from one end of town to the other might be wondering what on earth she was about, but that was the least of her concerns at the moment. Poor Janet. Poor Henrietta and Nathaniel. How must they be feeling? And Alex and the children.

Finally, standing in front of the police station on Dickson Street, Emma paused to catch her breath.

Despite having been involved in several suspicious deaths some years back, she had never been inside a police station. Pushing open the door, she stepped into a public waiting room.

Nathaniel and Alex were at the counter making demands of a steely faced officer. Nathaniel seemed to be asking to see Sergeant Donovan, while Alex wanted to see his wife. Henrietta was seated alone in a row of chairs along the back wall, a handkerchief to her face. Emma went straight to her.

"What has happened?" she asked, bending down, and putting her arms around the older woman.

Henrietta wept on her shoulder before gathering herself. Emma sat beside her, keeping an arm around her friend's shoulder.

"We'd barely opened this morning, and he came in, that Sergeant Donovan," she told her. "Walked right into the kitchen and arrested her for murdering her grandfather. Oh, Emma," she cried, "he put the handcuffs on her. Then he marched her down the street like some common criminal. I thought I was about to die there on the spot. To think she'd kill someone, and her own grandfather…"

Emma stared unseeingly across the room. This had to be Dr. MacArthur's call. He'd decided the blow to the head had caused the heart attack. But that was only an opinion. It wasn't a fact. There was only circumstantial evidence that Janet had delivered the blow. And the lack of blood. Emma drew in a sharp breath and sat taller. Surely the police hadn't found evidence of a cleanup. They'd have something to answer for if that were the case.

"Have they found any other evidence?" she asked.

"They found the piece of firewood when they searched the parlour this morning," Henrietta replied. "It was under his chair, so the Sergeant said."

Charity hadn't mentioned anything about a search. Even if the Sergeant hadn't told the woman what they'd found it would have been the decent thing for Charity to tell her they'd been there. Typical.

"And they're sure it was the piece of firewood he was hit with, are they?"

Henrietta nodded. "There are hairs and, and other matter on it."

Emma berated herself for not having Janey search the parlour yesterday. She'd allowed herself to be swept along by Dr. MacArthur's story of a possible cleanup. Though what would they have done with it? Hide it? It wouldn't have helped.

"There's no proof that Janet used it," she said now.

"Except that Miriam saw it in her hand."

"We need Jonathon Inglis. Perhaps he can get Janet out on bail while we try and figure this out." This was happening all too fast.

"Yes, yes, of course." Henrietta brightened and got to her feet. "I'd completely forgotten. Nat? Nat, we need Jonathan Inglis," she said approaching him at the counter. "He said he would defend Janet. Pro bono, he said. Can you go get him?"

"He said that? When did he say that?"

"Yesterday, at lunch."

Nathaniel looked between them, flustered and bewildered. Emma wondered if he'd relied on his father to make the decisions regarding life's issues, as Charity had, and that was why he was struggling now. With that thought came an even more troubling one. If Old Mr. Pickles had exerted greater control over his family than she realised, could his stubbornness over the will have been the final straw for Nathaniel? And now his daughter was at risk.

Nathaniel brushed his hand over his head. "Right, right, yes. That's, that's decent of him. A barrister. Of course, a barrister. I should speak to Samuel. He'd retain a barrister for us, so Mr. Inglis, yes, he was there, he knows all about it already, and..."

"Nat, please go and get him," Henrietta urged. "We'll stay here. Please hurry," She watched him leave the station. "He's in shock," she said. "He'll be himself again by and by."

"Who is Samuel?" Emma asked.

"The Pickles' attorney, Samuel Rasmussen. I did tell you about them. Kentish, Rasmussen and Foyle."

Probably something else she'd missed while her mind wandered, but Emma did remember the female Rasmussens she'd met at the Benevolent Society meeting. Was that only two days ago?

"Oh, Emma, I do hope he can help."

"Hush, let's wait and see." Emma led Henrietta back to the chairs and they sat.

Nathaniel was looking a little less flustered when he returned fifteen minutes later with Jonathan Inglis.

Jonathan carried a briefcase and looked every inch the confident barrister in his dark suit, black agate buttons winking on his vest. Emma could picture him in a court of law, holding the jury in thrall to his argument. He had the appearance at least. Whether he had the substance, she didn't yet know.

He approached the counter and presented his card to the officer, requesting to see his client, Mrs. Janet Naughton without delay. Minutes later a door opened, and he disappeared into the bowels of the station.

Alex and Nathaniel joined Henrietta and Emma on the chairs. Behind the counter, an officer cast an occasional glance their way, but no one spoke. Alex's face was white as he sat, hands drooped between his knees, head down. This wasn't a situation any of them had a precedent for.

"Mr. Pickles," Emma said addressing Nathaniel, "may I ask you some questions while we wait?"

"What do you want to know?"

"I'm sure Henrietta has told you that we believe Henry Collins came into the house with your father after lunch on Wednesday, and that they were arguing. I understand they have business dealings together, is that right?"

"Henry Collins. Of course. I was going to see him later today, but then... Do you think he might be involved in my father's death?"

"Well, the police need to speak to him at least, don't they? If he was indeed the person your father was speaking to. What was their involvement?"

"Henry Collins and my father owned two riverboats, the *Perseus*, and the *Parrot*, and three barges, *Allen*, *Oxford*, and *Maxine*. Both boats are working with a barge each. The *Maxine*, unfortunately, is rotting away on a sandbank downriver near Euston with a great hole in her hull, not worth salvaging."

"I see." It was a common enough story. "How are they doing, businesswise?"

"Not so well, now. Father was past managing the business, I'm afraid, and Collins never seemed to lift a finger. He leaves it up to the captains, neither of whom have the business experience or contacts, and it isn't their business to manage in any case. They rarely carry a full cargo either way these days."

"So, what might they have been arguing about?"

Nathaniel stroked his chin thoughtfully. "What indeed. There are rumours that Collins' business dealings are stretched for cash right now."

"I can vouch for that," Alex put in, looking up. "I've been chasing him for payment of his account for almost a year, and he keeps expecting more credit. He's a slippery fellow when he wants to be."

"Mmm. He might have been pressing Father to sell, or buy him out," Nathaniel said.

"And your father refusing?"

"Very likely," he said wryly.

"So, what happens to the riverboats now, do you know?"

"Collins will get full ownership, is my understanding."

"But that gives him a motive for your father's death."

"It does, it does. But surely…It's rather hard to believe, but I suppose, if he were desperate enough."

The door at the end of the waiting room opened and Jonathan Inglis came into view. All four of them were on their feet, expectant, but he was alone.

"I can't get bail, I'm sorry. It's a capital crime she's charged with after all. But you can visit for a few minutes, one at a time."

Henrietta, Alex, and Nathaniel looked at one another. "You go," Henrietta said to Alex. As he disappeared into the nether regions of the station in company with a police officer, Henrietta turned to Nathaniel. "He's beside himself. I couldn't make him wait any longer."

"Of course not," he said, touching her arm briefly. She and Henrietta sat again, and Nathaniel moved away and spoke quietly to Jonathon.

Emma realised the police still didn't know of Henry Collins' involvement on the day Old Mr. Pickles died, but Sergeant Donovan would no doubt brush her off if she spoke to him about it.

She stood and approached the men. "I'm sorry to interrupt, but we were just talking about Mr. Collins, and his visit to your father on Wednesday, Mr. Pickles. He needs to be questioned. You must inform Sergeant Donovan that he was there that day."

"What's this?" Jonathan asked. "There's someone else involved?"

"I was about to tell you," Nathaniel said, and did so.

"That's very interesting, indeed," Jonathon said, "and yes, the police must be informed about this Collins fellow." He asked to see Sergeant Donovan and was again escorted inside. Nathaniel nodded approvingly.

"Have you spoken to Sergeant Donovan this morning?" Emma asked him, wondering why the senior police officer wasn't in the front office dealing with the Pickles family personally.

"He was out here earlier, explaining to us that of course we believe Janet didn't kill her grandfather, families always think their loved one is innocent, but the evidence says otherwise, and there's nothing he can do about that. He's just doing the job the colonial government pays him to do, so he says." Emma supposed that was all good and proper, as long as he did the job diligently, given the consequences of getting it wrong.

It was some time before Jonathon reappeared, and when he did it was clear, from his tight-lipped expression, that he hadn't been successful. Again.

Chapter 11

Henry Collins Disappears

"I'M SORRY, MR. PICKLES," he said. "Sergeant Donovan doesn't see any point in chasing up this Henry Collins. He argues, firstly, that we only have the word of the maid that she heard someone come into the house with Mr. Pickles Snr, as no one actually saw him. Secondly, there's no evidence at all that this person, if he was there, is who Mrs. Berry claims him to be.

"But thirdly, and more damning, it is clear from the evidence and witness reports, that Mr. Pickles Sr was alive sometime later in the afternoon, after this person, if he ever existed, had apparently left the house."

Nathaniel rubbed his hand over his head. "I need to speak with Samuel Rasmussen. I'll go and do that right now."

"I'm sorry I've been unable to help, Mr. Pickles," Jonathon said again.

"You did your best. It might take a local man to deal with this. Someone with local connections."

Jonathon winced. Nathaniel went to speak briefly to Henrietta before hurrying away. Emma wondered if Jonathon's use of her name in his explanation to Sergeant Donovan had worked against him. The Sergeant seemed to be hostile to her involvement, or perhaps he just didn't like any lay person, especially a woman, butting in on his investigation.

"If the police won't speak to Henry Collins, then we need to, Mr. Inglis," Emma said. "He might be able to tell us something that will help Janet," she felt she was clutching at straws, but it was all she had. "But I doubt he will speak to me. I need someone to come with me, someone like yourself, with your law credentials." Even if they hadn't helped him with Sergeant Donovan.

"Why would you need to be involved in that conversation at all, Mrs. Berry? I understand you're a friend of Mrs. Pickles, but you seem to be taking on more than the role of a supportive friend."

"Henrietta asked me to be involved because of my past experience investigating several suspicious deaths. And…"

Jonathan Inglis' eyebrows rose. "Past experience?"

"I could tell you about that someday, Mr. Inglis, but we don't have the time right now. It's obvious the police aren't going to make any further enquiries, as they believe they've got the person responsible."

"That's true, from what Sergeant Donovan said when I spoke to him. The coroner is of the opinion the blow to the head caused the heart attack that killed Mr. Pickles Snr, and that Mrs. Naughton delivered the blow."

Emma was getting the distinct feeling that Dr. MacArthur wielded a great deal of authority in the town. "So, you agree that we must do our own investigating then, to reveal what really happened?"

"Well, my job in defending Mrs. Naughton will be to draw up an argument for the court, to counter the prosecution," he began.

"I suspect you might not have the job of defending her in court, Mr. Inglis. I suspect Mr. Pickles will have Mr. Rasmussen engage someone else for that task now, don't you?" Jonathon's mouth tightened. Emma felt sorry for the young man. "The ideal outcome would be for this to never reach court. It would be far better if we could find out what really happened and get Janet released. I don't believe the police have even thoroughly questioned anyone. They've just jumped to their own conclusion." With Dr. MacArthur's help, of course.

Jonathon nodded. "You're right. The police should have questioned everyone in the house more thoroughly, but they're so sure they have the culprit. I've seen it before. It's why I took up the law."

"You'll need to tell me about that sometime, as well," Emma said.

Alex returned to the waiting room at that moment, and Henrietta was escorted inside to visit Janet.

"How is she?" Emma asked him. If anything, Alex looked paler and more haggard than when he went in. His dark hair stood on end as if he'd been dragging his fingers through it, which he probably had.

"Frightened," he said. "And angry. I had to leave her there." His voice broke. Emma put her hand on his arm, as he gathered himself. "She trusts you'll sort this out, Emma. We both do. You will, won't you?" He looked at her imploringly.

"We will, Alex. Mr. Inglis and me. Won't we, Mr. Inglis?"

"We'll certainly try," Jonathan replied, if a trifle bemused. Emma thought he could have sounded a little more positive.

"Then might I suggest we get on and find Mr. Collins," Emma said. "We aren't doing any good just standing here. Can anyone tell me where he lives?"

"Two doors past the Exchange Hotel, which is two doors past my place," Alex told them, meaning his livery stable. Emma left a message for Henrietta telling her they had people to talk to, and she'd see her later. It was back to Hare Street.

Alex went with them, Emma's hand tucked under his arm. The walk was more sedate than the journeys she'd made up and down the street earlier in the morning.

"You two seem to know one another well," Jonathan commented as they walked. "Is there a family connection? Old friends?"

"My family owns a sheep property on the Murray and Alex worked on the adjoining property," Emma explained. "We didn't know one another very well there, just to say hello now and then, and talk horses."

"I worked in the stable."

"And then, he moved to town and ended up managing the livery stable, before marrying my friend and neighbour, Janet Pickles," Which mention of her name reminded them of where Janet was at that moment. Emma squeezed Alex's arm, and a silence descended that wasn't broken again until they reached Hare Street.

"Good luck," Alex said, before leaving them to return to his work. "We're relying on you." Emma tried not to think about what rested on their shoulders.

Mr. Inglis offered Emma his arm and they walked on past the Exchange Hotel, where a cab was depositing a couple with suitcases onto the footpath. The house they wanted turned out to be a single storey building with a neglected front yard, bare sand being the main feature.

Emma was about to turn into the path leading to the house, when ahead of them the front door slammed, and a tall man wearing a dark suit and a scowl, strode down the path and pushed his way past them.

"Was that our man?" Jonathon asked, as they watched him head down the street.

"No." Though Emma thought he might have been one of the men at the Society meeting who had accompanied Henry Collins.

"Well, let's hope we have better luck than he seems to have had."

A sign on the front door offered rooms to rent. Emma thought it probably only had about three available. A child of four answered the doorbell, followed quickly by a woman in her late twenties simply dressed in a plain black dress and white pinafore. Her thin face was flushed.

"Henry Collins?" she repeated when Jonathan asked if he was at home. She huffed. "If you're another one wanting money from him, you're out of luck. He packed a bag and took off two days ago, owing me for a weeks' rent and doing."

"Ah. I don't suppose you would know where he's gone?"

"He's not likely to be telling me, nor anyone else he owes money to, is he?

"No, I suppose not. Sorry to have troubled you." Jonathan raised his hat to the woman and half turned away.

"Did he leave any belongings behind?" Emma asked, stepping up and putting a hand on the door to keep it from closing.

"He did. A suit still in the 'robe, shirts and under-things in the wash. Why?"

"Well, that does suggest he's planning on return-ing, doesn't it?" Emma said. "Perhaps put them away and rent his room out. If he returns, you can use them to bargain for what he owes, and if he doesn't pay it, you have a right to sell them and get what you can. As for the room, he'll have to find somewhere else to live if you're full, or if you don't want him back."

The woman relaxed a little and almost smiled. "You're right. I'll do that. I've been so busy I haven't been thinking clearly."

Emma smiled back. "What was Mr. Collins wear-ing when he left?"

"Dark grey suit, homburg, pocket watch and chain. Although he might have to sell that." The sound of a baby crying reached them from somewhere in the house. The woman glanced back and was about to close the door.

"Do you know the man who was here just before we called in? He didn't look pleased."

"Mr. Laughlan. He and Mr. Collins had some busi-ness together I believe." The woman shrugged and closed the door.

"Does that help?" Jonathan asked.

"I don't know. Is Collins running from creditors, or because he killed Old Mr. Pickles?"

Emma wondered how much experience Jonathon Inglis had in questioning witnesses. Perhaps he'd spent the years since graduating in dealing with paperwork.

"So, where do you suppose this Collins fellow would have gone?" he asked.

"If he's left town in a hurry, as it appears, it will likely be by riverboat or train. And if Mr. Pickles didn't mention it when we were speaking earlier, it probably wasn't by boat as he'd have had to register as a passenger. For insurance purposes," she added, as Jonathon opened his mouth as if about to question that claim.

Emma directed them to Packenham Street, which was nearby. The railway station was partway down the street, toward the river and Dutch's slip. Jonathon had travelled to Echuca by train from Melbourne with Miriam and Grace, so wasn't completely unfamiliar with the area. Emma knew it well from some years ago.

There was still only one train into town and out each day, so it was simple enough to enquire if a short, stocky man, in a dark grey suit and homburg had taken a train ticket for the south either that morning or the day before.

"You may know him of course," Emma said to the stationmaster. "Mr. Henry Collins?"

The stationmaster looked from her to Jonathon. "Is this an official enquiry?" Jonathon produced his card. It had the desired effect, as the stationmaster nodded before returning it. "I do know the man. But

I haven't seen him for some time, and certainly not catching the train in recent days," he assured them.

They thanked him and walked back onto the street. Emma promised herself to find out what Jonathon Inglis' card actually said about him, but right now she was at a loss as to what to do next.

"He must be lying low somewhere," she puzzled. But where? She had no idea who he might trust enough to hide him. She should have asked Nathaniel more about the man.

"Could he have gone off on a boat under an assumed name?" Jonathon asked, as they stood pondering the problem.

Emma grabbed at the idea, but only for a moment. "I suspect he might be too well known to pass that off. Unless… It might be possible. We need to find out if either the *Parrot* or the *Perseus* have been and gone in the last two days."

"The who?"

"The two riverboats Mr. Collins has a financial interest in. He could have gone aboard one of them. The captains wouldn't ask awkward questions of the man who employs them." There wouldn't have been any expectation of paying the fare either. But that could only have happened if one of the riverboats was available. Had Henry Collins been that lucky? "Let's see. We'll take the short route to the wharf along the spur line."

"So, how well do you know this Henry Collins?" Jonathon asked, as they crossed Pakenham Street and trudged through the sand and tussocky grass that covered the space between the rail track and the river. Buildings backed onto the other side of the spur line. "You say he's well known in town?"

"I suppose he is. He's a businessman of some sort. I don't really know him at all. He spoke at a recent meeting of the Ladies Benevolent Society that I attended. Not a very pleasant man, by all accounts, but that is the only time I've seen him."

"Other than when you saw him walking off with the elderly Mr. Pickles on the day he died."

"Oh, yes, and then, of course."

"You did see him that time, didn't you?"

"Are you doubting my word, Mr. Inglis?"

"I'm just making sure I have my facts straight and wondering if your sighting of this man with Mr. Pickles Snr was a, um, a red herring intended to take suspicion from Mrs. Naughton."

Emma stopped and turned to stare at the man. "As in a lie, you mean."

"That's not what I said…"

"But it's what you meant, isn't it, that I made up the story of seeing them together? That I lied?"

Chapter 12

A Little Subterfuge

"YOU'RE A FRIEND of Mrs. Naughton, and of the Pickles family, Mrs. Berry," Jonathon explained. "It would be understandable if you wanted to divert suspicion, but if I'm to help with this I need to know the truth. You just said you'd only seen the man once. If you said that on the witness stand, the prosecuting attorney would be on to it in a flash."

The man was right. Unfortunately. Emma sighed, and continued walking.

"Alright. The second time I saw Henry Collins, he had just accosted Old Mr. Pickles as he left the Tea-room after lunch on Wednesday," Emma explained, "My maid, Janey, and I followed him out of the Tea-room and saw them walking along the street together in the direction of the Pickles' house. The Pickles' maid, Peggy, told Janey later that she heard Old Mr. Pickles come in talking with another man who said to him, 'you're being unreasonable.' Putting two and two together, and hoping it made four, it seemed reasonable to assume that the man who cam into the house with Mr. Pickles must have been Henry Collins."

"I see." Emma hoped he did.

They passed a rail car, dodging the crane that was being used to load it, and stepped onto the wharf. In the wharf office, they found that Nathaniel Pickles was still absent.

Emma enquired of Mr. Norman if either the *Parrot* or the *Perseus* had left the wharf any time from Wednesday afternoon. A quick consult of the registers, and he was able to tell them that of the riverboats that had left for downriver in the last two days, one had indeed been the PS *Parrot*.

"Was it carrying passengers by any chance, Mr. Norman?" Emma asked.

"Ah," he consulted the register again, and frowned. "There was a Mr. Craig listed."

Emma thought he sounded uncertain. "Did you see him?" Mr. Norman looked at her as if unsure as to whether he should provide any other information.

"We need a little help, Mr. Norman," she said. "A man needed for non payment of accounts may have left town rather hurriedly, and we were wondering if he might have taken passage on the *Parrot* under an assumed name."

"Oh, a debtor, is he?" Mr. Norman said. "Well, as it's you enquiring, Mrs. Berry, I didn't see the man, myself. Captain Nesbit provided the information. I thought it a little odd. He said to put the passenger's name down as Craig, salesman."

"Suggesting that it might not have been his real identity?" Jonathon asked.

Mr. Norman leaned forward. "I did wonder," he said quietly, "but it isn't my job to ask too many questions. I leave that up to the customs men." He tapped the side of his nose knowingly.

Emma thanked him, and she and Jonathon withdrew to discuss the matter.

"How do you think we should deal with this?" he asked her. "Is it possible to track a boat on the river?"

Emma explained how the captains kept in touch by telegraph from each town, and sometimes from the pastoral stations that had the telegraph connected. She knew her father had had it installed at Wirramilla recently.

"We could send a telegraph to Captain Nesbit asking him if his passenger was Henry Collins. The telegraph would follow him from place to place until it caught up with him."

"Would he admit to it though, if it were true?"

"That's the question, isn't it?" Emma agreed. "It might depend on whether his passenger was still on the boat. If he wasn't, if he'd left him somewhere along the way, he possibly would. And of course, telegraphs going from place to place aren't exactly confidential."

"So, they could warn Henry Collins that someone was onto him and send him deeper into hiding."

"It could." But was it a risk worth taking? The telegraph was the fastest way, indeed the only way, of tracking the man down with any speed. The police could do it, sending a message from station to station down the river. But the police weren't interested.

Emma considered the matter, idly noting the activity in the cargo shed as her gaze wandered around the space. She stopped as a familiar figure caught her attention. She hadn't seen him in years. A customs man. Aubrey Sinclair, known as the Weasel, as much for his sharp face as his sneaky manner. Both reminded those who knew him of that tiny animal, much maligned for its ability to sneak into chicken coops. As she watched him, checking packages and boxes, an idea popped into her mind. That would be a speedy way of finding someone. But dare she?

"He's very dedicated to his job," Emma told Jonathon, after explaining what she had in mind. "If you were to tell him that you suspect a man is travelling on the PS *Parrot* under an assumed name, he will be champing at the bit to investigate. Suspicion is his middle name."

Jonathon's lips twitched. "I thought you said his middle name was Weasel, Mrs. Berry."

"You can laugh," Emma told him. "He's a suspicious weasel of a customs officer." And a customs officer was the one person who could search a riverboat without cause.

"Are you sure you don't want to speak to him yourself, as you appear to know him quite well."

"Oh, he wouldn't take notice of a mere woman," Emma said airily, having no intention of explaining that her last encounter with the Weasel did not forge a friendship. If Sinclair had any friends. "Just flash that card of yours. He lives for intrigue. He sees law-breaking and smuggling everywhere, especially where it isn't."

"But I can't tell him I suspect this Craig person of smuggling. That would be a pure fabrication." Jonathon looked almost outraged at the very idea.

"I'm sure you could manage to suggest it without actually saying so, Mr. Inglis," Emma wheedled.

Jonathon huffed. "I'm beginning to see what I've let myself in for," he muttered.

Just as long as he didn't have second thoughts and pull out. Janet needed his help, and Emma suspected she did as well. She certainly wouldn't be able to get any help from Aubrey Sinclair herself. He'd probably laugh at her.

She watched as Jonathon approached the man in question, before quietly slipping out to the wharf. It wouldn't help their cause if Aubrey Sinclair suspected Jonathon had anything to do with her. There was a bench seat at the near end of the wharf. Jonathon would see her there when he came out of the shed. She sat down to wait in the warm spring sunshine.

In front of her, the PS *Sapphire* nudged its way into a space at the wharf, steam escaping the funnel in a hiss as the pressure was released from the boiler. Beyond it, a bevy of ducks and several black swans occupied the water closer to the opposite bank. Life was going on around her as normal. It hardly seemed right. Had Nathaniel Pickles been able to speak to Samuel Rasmussen? Perhaps the local attorney would have more sway with Sergeant Donovan, and get Janet released on bail. She was startled as Jonathon sat down beside her and realised, she'd all but dozed off in the sunshine.

"How did it go?" she asked, hoping he hadn't noticed she'd almost been asleep. "What is he doing?"

"I think it went rather well," Jonathon told her, clearly looking pleased, and perhaps a little surprised. "He's sending telegraphs downriver to Swan Hill to the customs office there, and to several other places beyond. He's asking the customs officers to apprehend this passenger and find out 'what his game is,' to use his words."

"Oh, well done. And how will we know if he finds him? Is he going to contact you?"

"Mr. Norman promised to tell Mr. Pickles, or to send a message to the Pickles' residence. Mr. Sinclair said it wasn't necessary, that he would be handling the matter. But I reminded Mr. Norman of what you'd said about the man being a debtor, and sort of hinted that I had a client involved who was owed money. He seemed to understand."

"Flashed that card of yours again, I suppose," Emma said. "I do believe you're enjoying this."

"Well, I suppose I am, at that. Considering most of what I've done previously has been from behind a desk, this is proving rather, well, liberating." Emma nodded. She understood the excitement of the chase, but this wasn't a game. Janet's future depended on them. "Did Aubrey Sinclair have any idea as to who this Mr. Craig might be?"

Jonathon shook his head. "I didn't make any suggestions on that score and neither did he. I kept it very hush hush. We'll just have to wait and see what he discovers now."

Emma rubbed her forehead. Wait and see wasn't her favoured way of doing things. And she was getting a headache.

"Are you feeling unwell, Mrs. Berry?"

"I believe I'm in desperate need of a cup of tea and sustenance," Emma said. It seemed a long time since breakfast, and she'd been walking half the morning.

"Well, we can soon fix that," Jonathan said, getting to his feet and offering his arm.

She directed him the short route to High Street, hoping Henrietta had managed to open the Tearoom. Fortunately, she had, helped by Alice, and Alice's sister Lena. Henrietta seated them at a table by the window and Lena soon delivered their tea.

Emma drank down a cupful and poured herself another, hoping the food wouldn't be too long. As if to remind her how long it had been since breakfast, her stomach rumbled.

"Have you lived long in town?" Jonathan asked, covering for Emma's embarrassment. "You did say earlier you'd grown up on a sheep property somewhere on the river."

For the next ten minutes they shared stories of their early years and drank more tea. Johnathan had lived all his life in Melbourne, eventually graduating from the University with a law degree and spending the obligatory three-year clerkship needed for admission to the bar. He'd spent another twelve months with the same law firm and was now taking some unpaid leave.

"I haven't decided yet whether to return to the company or to open my own office," he said as Lena delivered bowls of tomato soup, and crusty chicken salad sandwiches. "It isn't easy to set up in business unless you've already made a name for yourself."

"I suppose so," Emma agreed. She was trying to eat her soup without slurping but it was delicious, and she was very hungry. She interspersed the soup with mouthfuls of chicken sandwich. Some minutes later, her soup bowl empty and feeling much better, she put a half-eaten sandwich back on her plate.

"This is most frustrating," she commented.

"Pardon," Jonathan asked, somewhat startled as they'd been eating in silence for some minutes. "Is there something wrong with your lunch?"

"What? No, of course not. It's delicious, as usual. I mean, it's one thing to wait for answers to Aubrey Sinclair's telegraphs, providing we do hear anything, of course. But what if this mysterious Mr. Craig isn't Henry Collins?" Jonathon's eyebrows rose. "What if this Mr. Craig doesn't even exist? Henry Collins could have had Captain Nesbit register a mythical passenger to make people think it could be him, when he's actually hiding out right here in Echuca, or worse still, he's already in Melbourne. He could have had someone deliver him to a railway station further down the line where no one would recognise him."

She didn't want to believe the man could be out of reach already, but he'd had forty eight hours to make his escape, and time was of the essence.

Jonathon looked somewhat taken aback, but one thing she'd learnt from previous murders in the countryside was that the guilty party was promptly shipped off to the city to be dealt with. No country police station wanted their scarce cell space occupied with a permanent resident requiring three meals a day, cynical a thought as that might be. How long did they have before Janet was sent down to Melbourne?

"Do you know of some other avenue of enquiry?" Jonathon asked, clearly doubtful.

"Someone in town must know where Henry Collins has gone," Emma said, gesturing with her hand. "Someone must collect his mail and take his messages. He's a businessman after all. There must be other people he was involved with apart from Old Mr. Pickles. Who would know about that?"

"His agent, attorney?"

"Of course. Kentish, Rasmussen and Foyle." Emma took another bite of her sandwich, washing it down with more tea. It was cold. "Old Mr. Pickles' attorneys should know something. If they don't handle Mr. Collins business affairs themselves, they would know who does." Emma caught Lena's attention and asked her for a fresh pot of tea and was Henrietta free to speak to them for a few minutes.

Henrietta delivered the tea soon after. "Do you have some news?" she asked, pulling out a chair and sitting. Emma thought the poor woman had aged ten years in a matter of hours.

"Not yet, but we are following up on some ideas," Emma assured her. "Did Nathaniel manage to get in touch with Mr. Rasmussen this morning?"

"Yes, but he said he couldn't very well interfere in a police enquiry, and nor would he be able to get Janet out on bail."

"But the police aren't making any enquiries," Emma said, tapping the table in frustration. Henrietta strangled a sob in her throat, and Emma winced. She shouldn't have spoken out in that way in front of her.

She reached for Henrietta's hand and squeezed. "We'll get to the bottom of this," she assured her friend. "Did you see Janet?"

Henrietta nodded and dashed her hand across her eyes. "She's dealing with this better than we are, but I think that's because she's convinced herself you're going to sort this out, Emma." Oh, lordy. Not more pressure.

Emma had Jonathon tell Henrietta how he'd enticed Aubrey Sinclair to call in the customs men to find the mysterious Mr. Craig, aka Henry Collins. At least it brought a smile to Henrietta's face. She promised to tell Nathaniel. Emma thought he would enjoy the irony of it too, and she must remember to tell Daniel. Well, perhaps not. Until it was some time in the past, anyway. Henrietta returned to the kitchen, hopefully feeling a little brighter.

"We need to speak to Samuel Rasmussen," Emma said. "Mr. Pickles doesn't know Henry Collins has disappeared, so he won't have told Mr. Rasmussen, which means we can use that as an excuse to see him."

They finished their tea in silence, and Emma availed herself of the facilities. When she returned to the main room, Jonathan had paid for the meal and was waiting for her by the front door, tapping his hat against his leg. As they stepped out onto the street, Emma was accosted by Delia Rasmussen.

Chapter 13

A Request Refused

"Mrs. Berry, how lovely to see you again," Delia said. She turned to her companion. "Hannah, this is the lady I told you about who stood up to Henry Collins at the Society meeting the other day. Mrs. Berry, this is my friend Hannah Foyle. Our fathers are in business together."

"How terribly brave of you," Hannah said, extending her hand.

"Pleased to meet you, Miss Foyle," Emma said, noticing how both young women were eyeing Jonathan. "May I introduce Mr. Jonathan Inglis. This is Miss Delia Rasmussen and, as you heard, Miss Hannah Foyle. Mr. Inglis is affianced to Henrietta Pickles' niece, Miriam," she added, in order that there be no misunderstandings.

"Delighted to make your acquaintance, Mr. Inglis," Delia said offering her hand.

"Likewise," said Hannah.

"I had heard the Pickles were hosting family visitors," Delia went on. "Are you staying long in town Mr. Inglis?"

"We have no definite departure date as yet," Jonathan told her. Oh dear. There was definitely a little spark between these two. Best for Miriam if the visitors didn't linger long in town.

"And what," Delia asked prettily, "if I'm not presuming, are you and Mrs. Berry doing about town today?"

"Business, I'm afraid, Miss Rasmussen," Emma said, before Jonathan could speak. "And we really must be getting on. You are going into the Tearoom for lunch?"

"Yes, we are," Delia replied, pouting, apparently not used to having her questions unanswered.

"Then may I suggest the tomato soup and chicken salad sandwiches?"

"Well, thank you for the suggestion. Perhaps we will see you about town, Mr. Inglis?"

"That's quite possible, Miss Rasmussen. The town is not overly large. Good day to you both." He doffed his hat to them.

Emma took his arm and drew him across the street. A covered delivery cart was standing outside a shop, providing a convenient temporary cover from prying eyes. Unfortunately, it also prevented them from seeing who was standing on the other side of it.

"Well, well, Mrs. Daniel Berry if I'm not mistaken." Aubrey Sinclair stood before them. Emma always thought of the Dicken's character, Uriah Heep, when she saw him, although there was nothing humble about Aubrey Sinclair. Her heart sank. He was without a doubt the very last person she wanted to see her with Jonathan.

He looked her companion up and down. "What is this?" he said looking back at Emma, his eyes gleaming with suspicion. He might not have been rubbing his hands right now, but his demeanour suggested that he could be considering doing so, if he discovered he'd caught her out in something. "What are you up to? What have you got to do with this Craig business, eh? Is this some wild goose chase you've sent me on? Because if it is, you and that husband of yours are going to rue the day you crossed me. I never for a moment believed that mattress was put out by mistake."

"It was a mistake, Mr. Sinclair. An honest mistake on my part." Which was perfectly true. She hadn't known what Daniel and Shorty had cooked up between them, but she had enjoyed that they'd bested the man. "But that's way in the past."

"That's as maybe. What's this business you're involved in now, eh?"

"That's business between you and me, Mr. Sinclair," Jonathon said. "Have you heard something already?"

Sinclair looked torn between suspicion and his desire to boast about his success. Emma huffed, as if impatient at being held up, and walked on past him, leaving the men to talk. She stopped just within hearing distance and pretended to be searching in her bag.

"We have, of course," Sinclair said, dropping his voice. "We know our business in the customs service. We've learned the PS *Parrot* passed through Swan Hill without a passenger."

That news was a mixed blessing. Did it mean the passenger had been dropped off somewhere earlier, or that there never had been a passenger?

"That's impressive," she heard Jonathon tell him. "The police couldn't have got that information any quicker. Has anyone spoken to the Captain?"

"Not yet, but they will, they will. We've a temporary customs post set up at, ah, along the way."

Emma fidgeted with her gloves. "I really need to be getting on, Mr. Inglis. If you don't mind."

Sinclair snorted. Emma knew she was being rude. She just hoped Jonathon understood why.

"Of course, ma'am," he said. "Thank you, Mr. Sinclair. I hope the rest of your investigation is as successful and prompt." He joined Emma. She took his arm, walking on without a backward glance or a goodbye.

"Whew. I hope he believes I had no interest in all that," Emma said, when they were out of earshot. "Otherwise, he could make Daniel's life miserable."

"You couldn't have looked more disinterested if you'd tried," Jonathon assured her. "But what was that about a mattress? First, you're avoiding Henry Collins, and now I learn you've had a run in with a customs officer over a mattress. Is this normal for life in these parts? Or is it just normal for you?"

Was he laughing at her? But in a teasing way, she decided. He could be worse company. "As you just heard me tell Aubrey Sinclair," she said, copying his light tone, "I had nothing to do with the mattress mix up. The one that was supposed to be put out on the riverbank contained opium, and he was planning on burning it. Our crewmen put out the wrong mattress, that was all."

"One that didn't contain opium, I presume. And one that wouldn't cause a rather, let us say, interesting result, if it had burnt."

"Exactly, and very sensible."

"Mmmh. And I presume your avoidance of Henry Collins had to do with what Miss Rasmussen mentioned, about you speaking out against something he said at a meeting recently."

"That is correct as well. But those two incidents are some ten years apart, Mr. Inglis, in case you think I make a habit of getting into scrapes." She didn't wait for a comment. "But getting back to the matter we are concerned about right now, it appears we are no further forward to locating this Craig person."

"No, but you have to admit, Mrs. Berry, that your Mr. Sinclair has got onto the matter with admirable promptness."

"Please don't ever refer to him as 'my' Mr. Sinclair ever again, Mr. Inglis," Emma told him, in no uncertain tone. "That would be pushing a friendship to breaking point."

"Point taken, ma'am." Emma suppressed a giggle, turning it into a cough. She could see why Miriam was so enamoured of him. She couldn't help feeling though that Delia Rasmussen would be a better match.

Kentish, Rasmussen and Foyle occupied a two-storey building on Heygarth Street not far from Dr. MacArthur's Surgery. Jonathan held the door for Emma to enter. There was no one waiting in the public room, and the person behind the desk was a young man busy with paperwork. The name plate on the desk declared him to be Marcus Thrum. A clerk doing double duty, Emma supposed. She let Jonathan approach and ask to see Mr. Rasmussen.

"Do you have an appointment?" Mr. Thrum asked doubtfully, reaching for a register.

"No, but we would appreciate very much if we could speak to him about the death of a client of his, Mr. Augustus Pickles, and the subsequent arrest of Mr. Pickles granddaughter on the suspicion of murder," Jonathan said.

Mr. Thrum's eyes widened. "Your name, please?"

"Jonathan Inglis," he said, handing over his card, "representing Janet Naughton, the woman accused." Mr. Thrum's eyes flicked toward Emma. "And Mrs. Emma Berry." If Mr. Thrum wondered what part Emma was playing in this, Jonathan didn't enlighten him.

"Thank you. Please take a seat, and I will enquire if Mr. Rasmussen is available." He disappeared through a door at the back of the room, and very shortly returned.

"Mr. Rasmussen will see you," he said, and led them down a hall past closed doors, and the sound of one of the new typewriting machines Emma had read about. At least the firm seemed to be up to date.

Mr. Samuel Rasmussen proved to be a man in his late fifties, mid-height as he stood to greet them, and fit for someone his age who sat behind a desk. Emma imagined he rode for exercise as he had a good colour. Not someone who spent all his time behind a desk, anyway. His manner, when he greeted them and invited them to sit, was friendly, although his grey eyes were a little disconcerting as he sized them up.

Mr. Rasmussen already knew of Janet's arrest, having heard from Nathaniel Pickles, but Jonathon's request for his help in locating Henry Collins surprised him. At the mention of the man's name, Mr. Rasmussen's gaze had flicked to Emma for a brief moment. If she'd wondered at all if he'd heard from his wife or daughter about her confronting the man at the Society meeting, she felt that had been confirmed.

"Mr. Pickles did inform me that Henry Collins may have been at the house in company with Mr. Pickles Snr on the day. Now you say he's disappeared? Do you have reason to believe he may have been involved in my client's death?" Mr. Rasmussen asked. It was a straightforward question. Jonathan hesitated for a moment, as if searching for the right words. Emma jumped in.

"We really can't say at the moment, Mr. Rasmussen," she said. "But we've just discovered that Mr. Collins left his residence in a hurry later that afternoon, owing his landlady for his room and not informing her where he was going, or when he expected to return."

"Yes, well, in that case, locating and interviewing him should be a matter for the police."

"Yes, it should," Jonathon said. "But when I spoke to Sergeant Donovan this morning and informed him of the possibility that Mr. Collins' was in the house at the time, he told me they had the person responsible in custody, based on the coroner's report and witness evidence."

"Surely if Mr. Collins had been present when Mr. Pickles Snr collapsed, he would have called for help," Mr. Rasmussen argued.

"He could have panicked," Jonathon suggested, "especially if they were arguing and that caused the heart attack."

"Or he'd hit him on the head with the piece of fire-wood," Emma put in.

Mr. Rasmussen raised his eyebrows at that. "That seems rather extreme," he said mildly.

"But someone did, Mr. Rasmussen, didn't they?" Emma replied, wondering why he wasn't more engaged in the matter. "And more likely a man he was in business with than his own granddaughter." Mr. Rasmussen's fingers tapped his desk.

"Sir, it's possible Henry Collins took passage on the PS *Parrot* Wednesday evening," Jonathon said, "using the name Craig. We already have the customs service looking for him, but that could be a complete dead end if it turns out to not be him. So, we need to speak to people he knows, perhaps has business dealings with, who may have a better idea where to find him."

Mr. Rasmussen clicked his tongue. "I understand. However, I'm reluctant to give you names and draw others into this sordid affair. Of course, if the police were making the request, it would be a different matter altogether, but I can see why they feel they have the culprit in hand already. Hmm. What I can do is make some enquiries myself and see what I can discover. I'm sorry Nathaniel Pickles didn't inform me of Henry Collins disappearance when we spoke earlier today."

Emma wanted to remind him that Nathaniel didn't know Henry Collins was missing at that time, may still not know, but managed to keep her mouth shut. Just.

"I don't believe that man has ever handled a murder case before in his entire life," Emma said, frustration bubbling, when they were once more walking down High Street. "He believes Janet killed her grandfather and isn't prepared to lift a finger to help prove otherwise. He prefers to blame a woman than even think a fellow man could be guilty of such a crime." She wanted to stamp her foot but knew she'd look childish if she did.

What did Samuel Rasmussen base that belief on? Were they all under the thrall of Dr. MacArthur? No doubt they moved in the same tight social circle and hosted one another at dinner. She could feel her blood pressure rising at the unreasonableness of it all.

"I wonder if we can find that man we saw leaving Henry Collins' place?" Jonathon said, ignoring her outburst. Emma suspected he was afraid she might end up making a scene if he gave her words the slightest encouragement. "Laughlan, I think his name was. Mr. Pickles should know of him."

Of course. That Mr. Laughlan was an obvious person to speak to about Henry Collins. She needed to calm down. She was too worked up to think clearly.

"Can I leave that to you?" she said after a minute or two had passed in silence, and she felt she could speak more calmly. "It's time I spoke to Miss Charity Pickles and your future mother-in-law. I really need to develop a proper timeline of what everyone was doing on that Wednesday."

She'd been going about this whole enquiry back to front. A timeline for those in the house should have been one of the first things to do, but learning the result of the autopsy, and then the promising discovery of Henry Collins' presence had led them down a different path. She hoped they hadn't been wasting their time.

Chapter 14

Talking to the Pickles Ladies

IT WAS DECIDED to detour by the wharf first, as it was closer, and see if Nathaniel was there. When they found he was, Emma waited on the bench where she had sat that morning, leaving Jonathon to speak to him about Mr. Laughlan. It had already been a long day.

"I don't know if this news is of any use or not," Jonathon told her, when he joined her some minutes later. "But Evan Laughlan has taken passage to Toorangabbie Station on a boat that left the wharf just an hour ago."

"Toorangabbie? That's just fifty miles downriver. I wonder what his connection is there?" She knew the Weaver family, whose property it was. "Did Mr. Pickles know anything about his dealings with Henry Collins?"

"Not directly. He believes they have investments in common in various activities. "

"Mmmh, investments that might have gone wrong, if Mr. Laughlan's demeanour this morning was anything to go by. So, another dead end."

"Certainly no help in locating Henry Collins."

"No."

"You sound tired. Is more tea needed?" Jonathon asked.

"That, and something positive to happen."

"I can second that, on both counts. I suppose we should attend to the interviews with Miriam's family."

"Yes." But neither of them, it seemed, were in a hurry to move. Across on the further bank, a fisherman cast a line into the water, while behind him a wagon could be seen through the trees, moving toward the bridge further upstream. To add to the rural idyll, a riverboat came into sight from downriver, smoke pouring from its chimney stack, watery ripples catching the sun as they radiated out down its length.

"There could be worse places to live," Jonathan commented.

A group of cockatoos arrived overhead, screeching noisily as they settled in a tall river gum nearby.

Emma laughed. "It has it's downside."

"They're called a crackle, you know," Jonathon mused.

"What are?"

"A group of cockatoos. And a gathering of crows is a murder."

Emma winced. She didn't need to be reminded of murder. "Are you a twitcher, Mr. Inglis?"

"Not as such. A twitcher will travel miles to mark a bird off his list. I don't keep a list, but I do take photographs. There've been some promising developments in photography in recent years. It has uses for the law, too."

"Oh yes, you can photograph people in the act of committing a crime, now," Emma said.

"Sarcasm is the lowest form of wit, Mrs. Berry. You really are in need of tea."

"Well, let's see if we can get one at the Pickles' place, then," she said resignedly, getting to her feet.

Five minutes later they were turning into Connelly Street.

"I've just had a thought," Emma said. "Could we please not mention the possibility of Henry Collins' having been in the house? I would like to learn about everyone's movements on Wednesday first. Someone may have seen or heard him, and if they mention it, that's fine, but I don't wish to influence their memories of the day. We can tell them about him afterwards."

Jonathan looked at her thoughtfully. "You have something in mind?"

"I just think it good practice not to put ideas in people's heads," Emma said, not wanting to say more. The trouble was, she didn't feel she could rule out anyone who had been in the Pickles' house on

Wednesday afternoon, and she didn't want anyone grabbing at a possible new suspect to divert attention from themselves. It was enough that Jonathon knew about him.

Peggy let them into the house, and Miriam appeared at once from the parlour.

"Jonathan, where have you been? I was expecting you back hours ago," she greeted him, her voice querulous.

"We've been attending to Janet's defence," he replied, hanging his hat on the hall stand and shrugging out of his jacket. "Tea would be welcome right now."

Miriam glanced at Emma, her expression unreadable. "Of course. Tea in the parlour," she told Peggy.

"Yes, Miss." No please or thank you, Emma noticed. She wondered if Miriam always treated servants in that manner or if she was following Charity's example. It said something about her, either way.

Jonathon ushered them both into the parlour. The first thing she noticed was that Old Mr. Pickles' wing-backed chair had been moved to the back corner of the room. Grace was sitting in an armchair by the fireplace, where a small fire was burning. She had a book on her lap.

Open magazines and newspapers were strewn across the low table in front of the sofa where Charity sat, in stark contrast to it's condition when Old Mr. Pickles ruled the parlour. Miriam joined her aunt there and picked up one of the magazines.

"How is poor Janet?" Grace asked. So, it was 'poor Janet' now that the threat of the family absconding and the house being sold had been put to rest. She imagined Nathaniel would have updated his sisters when he came to collect Jonathon to attend at the police station that morning. It already seemed a long time ago.

"Still in jail," Jonathon told her, as he indicated one of the two armchairs beside the sofa for Emma. She had a view from there of everyone in the room. "The police won't allow her out on bail."

"Well, why should they when she killed Grandfather?" Miriam said, not looking up.

"She hasn't been convicted yet, Miriam," Jonathon told her quietly, as he took the armchair beside Emma.

"I'm sorry," Miriam said, at once contrite, "but I never got the chance to know my grandfather properly."

"Isn't there anything you can do?" Grace asked.

"We've spoken to an attorney, Mr. Samuel Rasmussen. He is, er, making enquiries."

"Mr. Rasmussen is our family attorney," Charity said, "but what sort of enquiries can he be making? No one was in the house except us."

No one disagreed. They either didn't know about Henry Collins' visit or weren't admitting to it, although she didn't know why they wouldn't if they knew he'd been there. That was the trouble with murder. You found yourself not trusting anyone. When Jonathon didn't comment, Emma jumped in before Charity could make something of the silence.

"We need to clarify the timeline of events on Wednesday, Miss Pickles. We need to muddy the waters. Create doubt. Regardless of what you might think of Janet, I'm sure you can't like the idea of having a murderer in your family."

"I should think not, but how do we go about creating doubt? Are you expecting us to lie? Because I can tell you now, that isn't going to happen."

"Of course not. Just tell me what you were doing on Wednesday afternoon, all of you," Emma said looking around the room, "minute by minute. It's the only way we're going to figure our what really happened."

"I'm game," Grace said, after a moment, looking to Charity.

"Well, I've certainly nothing to hide."

"We haven't either," Miriam agreed, "have we Jonathon?"

"That's right. Please go ahead, Mrs. Berry," Jonathon told her.

Emma took a notebook and pencil from her bag. "Can anyone tell me what time your father returned from lunch?" she asked, opening to a fresh page.

Looks were exchanged. "I've no idea," Grace replied.

"Did no one hear him come in?" Heads were shaken. "All right, where were you in the house from twelve noon? Mrs. Hewitt?"

"In the morning room. Charity and I had lunch there after father had gone out, but I didn't hear him come in."

"And where is the morning room located?" Emma asked. She'd never been in that room during the time she had stayed at the boarding house, didn't even know such a room existed in the place.

"It's at the back, on the other side of the kitchen," Charity told her. "It's the room we use all the time, our private sitting and dining room. Guests aren't allowed there."

Well, that explained that. It also explained why they might not have heard their father let himself into the house. Interesting though, that they now seem to have reclaimed the parlour.

"Can you hear the doorbell from there?"

"Yes, it rings in the kitchen, and at the top of the stairs, in case no one is downstairs at the time."

Emma did a quick sketch of the layout for her own benefit. "So, all four of you were in the morning room..."

"No, Jonathon and I were out," Miriam corrected. "We went for a walk and bought fish and chips from a little place near the wharf."

"Fish and fried potato eaten out of newspaper. Barbaric, I call it," Charity said.

"It's very popular in Melbourne right now," Miriam told her. "Some Greek in Sydney came up with the idea."

"Well, what else can you expect from foreigners."

"So, when did the two of you return after lunch?" Emma asked.

Jonathon answered for them. "It was about half past one."

Miriam nodded her agreement. "I looked in at the parlour when we came in and said hello to Grandfather, but he must have been asleep because he didn't answer. I went and freshened up, and then we sat in the morning room for a while."

"Were you all there at that time?"

"Peggy and I were upstairs for some time, springcleaning one of the guest rooms," Charity put in. "I'm not taking bookings while we have family visiting so it's a good time to get the odd job done. Then we went down to the kitchen to do the baking for afternoon tea."

"Alright, let's back up a minute. Were you in the morning room when Miss Hewitt and Mr. Inglis came back?"

"Yes. I sat in the morning room after lunch, Peggy cleaned up in the kitchen, and Jonathan and Miriam came back and joined us."

"You sent Peggy to the dining room earlier too, to throw out the flowers," Grace reminded her. Emma relaxed. She'd been wondering how she could introduce that if no one mentioned it. She wasn't supposed to know what Peggy had been doing, and the maid's whereabouts had needed to be confirmed. "Perhaps she went into the parlour and hit Father over the head while she had the chance," Grace suggested.

Charity gave what could only be described as a snort. "Don't be ridiculous, Grace. She had no reason to do anything of the sort."

"You don't always know what's going on around you," Grace said.

"Well, you would know about that, wouldn't you?"

Jonathon cleared his throat and both women settled to glaring at one another.

"So, what time would you have gone to the kitchen for the baking?" Emma asked Charity, after a moment.

"Tcht." This was obviously becoming a real chore. "I suppose we would've been in the kitchen by about half past two, perhaps a little earlier."

Which suggested that whoever was visiting Old Mr. Pickles had left by then, otherwise they would have heard the front door, or the parlour door, opening and closing, and possibly heard voices. Unless, of course, the old man was already dead and the visitor was sneaking out very, very quietly. Emma thought it more likely to indicate that only family members were in the house by that time.

"Thank you. Mrs. Hewitt, were you in the morning room all afternoon?" Emma asked.

"I was. I was reading," Grace said, holding up the book she had in her lap. "Well, re-reading really. I just love Trollope's Barchester novels."

"I've enjoyed them as well, Mrs. Hewitt," Emma said. "He's one of my favourite authors." Grace gave a small smile. "So, you didn't go upstairs, or into the parlour at any time?"

Grace shook her head, and Charity made another tutting sound. Was she annoyed that her sister wasn't helping out around the house? Emma felt that Charity's constant disapproval must get on the nerves of those who had to live with it day by day. It was bad enough for an hour or two.

Emma turned to Miriam. "So, what did you do between half-past-one and three that afternoon, Miss Hewitt?"

Miriam put a finger to her cheek as she considered. "Jonathan and I stayed in the morning room for a while. We chatted until Aunt Charity went upstairs, then we played several hands of single dummy whist. Mum was reading. Then I went to see if grandfather was awake. I wanted to speak to him."

"Did you go with her, Mr. Inglis?"

"No, I stayed in the morning room and read the papers."

"I see. So was your grandfather awake when you went to speak to him?"

"No, he was asleep." Miriam let out a long sigh. "So, I popped out for a walk. I didn't go far, just down the street, looked at the river for a bit, and came back in."

"And you're sure he was asleep?"

"Well, when I spoke his name, he sort of stirred a little, and then snored. I waited a moment, but he didn't wake up."

"So, it would have been about half past two when you went to speak to him?"

"Or a bit earlier, even," Miriam said.

"I didn't see her leave the morning room," Charity said, "so she must have gone to the parlour before I came downstairs."

Emma nodded. "Does anyone know when he sent the note to Janet?"

She was met with blank looks. "If there was a note," Charity said, "he would have had Peggy take it. But she didn't step out to deliver a note that afternoon. She was in the house working."

"So how else would it have been delivered?"

"I've no idea, which is why I don't believe it existed. I mean, once upon a time, when he was fit and well, Father would go out and deliver his messages in person, or he'd pay one of the lads on the street a halfpenny to do it. But these days, lunch at the Tearoom was as much as he could manage, and somedays not even that."

"But he did go to the Tearoom for lunch Wednesday," Grace said, "so he could have found a lad to deliver the note to Janet while he was out, couldn't he?"

"So why didn't he just speak to Janet while he was there?" Charity said, triumphant. Why not, indeed.

Chapter 15

Emma Sees The Light

"ALRIGHT, DID ANYONE see or hear Janet come in?" Emma asked.

"I did," Miriam volunteered. "I was in the kitchen after coming back from my walk."

Charity sniffed. "I can vouch for that. You kept getting in our way. And I always hear the front door from the kitchen. The sound echoes down the hall." She sent Emma a sharp glance. The woman didn't forget anything, either, it seemed.

"When I heard her at the front door," Miriam said, ignoring her aunt's comment, "I peeked out into the hall and saw her go into the parlour. I followed a few minutes later, when she didn't come straight back out. I thought Grandfather must be awake. Oh," her hands went to her face. "If only I'd gone straight in. I could have stopped her killing him." Jonathan got to his feet and went around to the sofa to comfort her.

"You've got to stop blaming yourself, sweetheart."

"I'm sorry," Emma said, "but I need to know. What did you see when you went into the parlour?"

Jonathon gave her a look that suggested he thought her insensitive, but she needed to hear it firsthand. Miriam shuddered and seemed to force herself to answer.

"Janet was standing there beside Grandfather's chair with the piece of firewood in her hand. She was frowning at him. I asked her what was going on and she said she didn't think he was well. I went to look at him, and I could see at once he was dead. That's when I screamed."

Emma wondered if Miriam's scream may have been more about frustration than anything else. Her grandfather wouldn't be amending his will in her mother's favour now.

"We all came running when Miriam screamed," Grace said. "Charity sent Peggy to fetch Nathaniel, and then Henrietta came. I was devastated. I'd spoken to Father just that morning, and he told me he would make things right. Then here he was, dead, and nothing will ever be right again."

"He told you he would be changing his will, Mrs. Hewitt?"

"Yes. Well, not in those exact words, Mrs. Berry. He said he would make it right. I guess that's why he asked Janet to come and see him."

"And how did you know he'd been hit on the head?" Emma asked.

"It was Nathaniel," Charity said. "That's when Miriam started making accusations." Exactly what Henrietta and Janet had said.

"Janet was the only one who'd been in the parlour after I'd seen him asleep," Miriam said. "And she had that piece of firewood in her hand. No one else could have done it."

"EMMA, YOU'VE got to eat," Daniel said over dinner that evening, as Emma pushed the food around her plate.

She had no appetite. Nothing further had been heard about the customs search for Mr. Craig, and after hearing what Miriam had to say, Emma couldn't see how talking to Henry Collins, should they even find him, was going to change anything. Old Mr. Pickles had still been alive, if asleep, later in the afternoon.

"I know you're worried," Daniel went on, "but not keeping your strength up isn't going to help."

"I know you're right, but knowing that doesn't help either," Emma said, poking her fork into a juicy piece of fish and staring at it. "Henrietta said Janet is doing okay, and she's taking meals to her, but Alex is beside himself, and the kids can tell something is wrong, but they don't understand. They just want their mother."

She knew all this because she'd called in at the Tea-room as it was getting dark, after she'd left the Pickles' house. Henrietta told her she wasn't opening over the weekend, loss of business or not. It was just too stressful. Don't forget to look after yourself, Emma had reminded her. She grinned wryly to herself now. Take your own advice, she chided and forced herself to eat the food on her fork.

After dinner they settled themselves in the parlour, Emma with a cup of tea and Daniel with a tot of whiskey, leaving Janey and Abe in the kitchen having their own meal. Darcy was engaged in building a tower of blocks on the floor, determined to do better than Jemmy had at his last attempt.

"I want to visit Janet tomorrow morning," Emma said, breaking the silence.

"And talk to Sergeant Donovan?"

"I guess." He knew her too well, though she doubted anything she said to the Sergeant would change anything. And what could she say, in any case?

"Would you like some company?"

Emma smiled at him. "It wouldn't hurt."

"We're still going upriver for that picnic Sunday," Daniel said. "Is there anyone you'd like to invite along?"

"Oh." The very thought of a Sunday outing with her friend stuck in jail didn't sit right.

"We are still going," Daniel told her, reaching for her hand. "You need a break too."

Emma swallowed and fiddled with the teaspoon on her saucer as she considered what to say. "We could take Janet's kids, I suppose. Give them a nice day out. Winnie, their nanny, would no doubt be happy to come. Perhaps Alex will be able to spend time with Janet on Sunday."

She couldn't imagine Janet or Alex wanting the children to see their mother in a jail cell. She couldn't begin to imagine a leave taking in those circumstances. It tore her heart apart at the thought. She couldn't see Henrietta or Nathaniel wanting to come either, and she wasn't about to ask Charity, or Grace, and have them niggling at one another all day.

"Jonathon and Miriam perhaps," she said, "as I don't suppose they've been on a riverboat before. They might enjoy it. And Janey and Abe, of course."

"Of course."

Emma sighed. Perhaps something would happen tomorrow to end this nightmare.

"WE WISH TO SEE Janet Naughton," Daniel told the officer behind the counter when he and Emma arrived at the police station early next morning, having left Darcy with Abe and Janey for an hour.

"Doesn't everyone," the man grumbled. Emma noted the name on his police badge.

"A great many people care about her, Constable Smith," she said.

"Lucky for some. Wait here while I check." He disappeared through a door on the side. A few minutes later, Sergeant Donovan appeared, shadowed by the Constable.

"Mrs. Berry. Captain," the Sergeant said, his acknowledgement of Daniel delayed by the blink of an eye.

"Sergeant," Daniel responded, his tone cool. Emma almost rolled her eyes. What on earth was that about?

"The police have better things to be doing than ferrying visitors back and forth to the cells all day," Sergeant Donovan said.

"I'm quite sure you do, Sergeant," Emma shot back. "Like finding out who really did hit Old Mr. Pickles on the head. How are you doing with that?"

"We have the person responsible."

"No, you don't." She and Sergeant Donovan stared at one another, neither giving in.

Daniel cleared his throat. "So, may we see her, Sergeant?"

Sergeant Donovan broke eye contact with Emma and nodded to Constable Smith, who escorted them to the cells. Emma hadn't seen behind the scenes in the police station before. It was a depressing sight, but she imagined they could have been worse. The police station was only a few years old, so the cells were relatively clean.

A narrow bed attached to the wall, a thin mattress, a blanket, and a lidded bucket in the corner were the only items in Janet's cell, apart from Janet herself, who was sitting cross-legged on the bed playing solitaire.

Constable Smith unlocked the cell for Emma to enter. Janet untangled her legs and stood, and she and Emma hugged.

"I'll wait out here," Daniel said, leaning back against the wall of the corridor and crossing his arms. Constable Smith looked about to object, but took one look at Daniel, relocked the cell and went away.

"Just in case the Sergeant gets any funny ideas," Daniel told them. Emma made a mental note to ask him what contact he'd had with Sergeant Donovan in the past, but she felt better for his being on the outside. Being locked in was already making her twitchy.

"Have you solved it yet, Emma," Janet asked, sitting back on the bed and pushing the cards out of the way.

"Not yet, I'm sorry," Emma said, sitting beside her in the cleared space. "We have to hear what Henry Collins has to say." If they could find him. If he had anything useful to add, like a confession. She forced herself not to show how hopeless she was really feeling. She was here to give her friend hope. "Mr. Inglis has been very helpful, and we have the customs men looking for Henry Collins. How are you holding up?"

"I'm okay. I'm looking at it like a holiday, though I'd prefer to be by the seaside with Alex and the kids." Her voice wobbled.

"Oh, Janet." Emma hugged her again. "Don't give up. It isn't over yet, and everyone's pulling for you."

"I know. Thank you. I do appreciate what everyone is doing."

"I spoke to your aunts, and your cousin, about what they were doing on Wednesday afternoon. Anyone of them could have popped into the parlour at some time. Charity and Peggy were upstairs for a while, and Grace was in the morning room. Then Miriam went in to speak to your grandfather, but he was asleep."

They all had stories of where they'd been during that early afternoon, but any one of them could be lying.

"But tell me, have Grace and Charity always been so at odds with one another? There's a lot of anger there, especially from Charity."

"They've been like that for as long as I've known them. It started a long time ago, according to Mum. Aunt Grace married Aunt Charity's lover. She's never forgiven either of them. It's why I've only seen Aunt Grace a handful of times in my life before this visit."

"Little wonder Charity's so bitter."

Janet nodded. "Even though they rarely saw one another, they seemed to just take up where they'd left off with their snide remarks. They were going at it over dinner on Monday night as well. It wasn't a very pleasant meal even before Grandfather made his announcement."

Something stirred in Emma's mind. "Do you think…"

"Time's up," Constable Smith's voice interrupted them as he unlocked the cell door. Emma gave Janet one last hug and walked out, feeling sick because she was glad she could. Daniel put his arm around her shoulder, and they returned to the waiting room. Nathaniel and Henrietta Pickles were just coming in with Alex.

"More visitors." Emma said.

Constable Smith rolled his eyes, but she could see his heart wasn't in it. This was probably better than locking up drunks, and even policemen had to have hearts. Most of them, anyway.

He escorted Alex to the cells to see Janet. Emma sat with Henrietta, while Daniel asked Nathaniel about some work that was rumoured to be planned for the wharf.

"Are you still intent on not opening the Tearoom over the weekend?" Emma asked, with one ear on the men's discussion.

"Yes, but," she shook her head, "I don't know if I'll ever be able to open it again, Emma. It won't be the same without Janet, and the children are going to need me."

Emma's stomach churned at what she was hearing. Henrietta had given up. She was planning life without her daughter.

"I've had to refuse a booking from Anna Marshall," she went on. "She wanted to hire the Tearoom for a morning tea to celebrate volunteers and charity workers. It's just the sort of event Janet and I loved to do ...." Henrietta's voice went on, but Emma's mind had drifted off.

Anna Marshall. Henrietta had mentioned her at the Society meeting. A cousin or something of Henry Collins. And crows. Jonathon had mentioned crows yesterday. But why would Anna Marshall's name remind her of that?

The last time she'd seen crows en masse they'd been attacking a small orchard of almond trees, and the owners were laying netting over the trees to protect the crop. She could still picture the men with ladders and long poles, the crows cawing as they were forced to abandon a tree or be caught under the net as it was manhandled over. She didn't know how effective the nets would have been. Crows were extremely clever. It hadn't been that long ago, had it? On one of her last trips on the *Mary B,* she seemed to remember.

Oh, that was where she'd met Anna Marshall. That's right. Anna was visiting her sister. They'd stayed long enough for Daniel and the crew to help with the netting and been treated to a nice afternoon tea. They hadn't been in a hurry. They hadn't far to go to reach Echuca because they were at...

"Toorangabbie," Emma cried. "He's at Toorangabbie. Of course. She's his cousin. Daphne Weaver is Henry Collin's cousin. She's Anna Marshall's sister. That's why he's there. That's why Evan Laughlan's gone there."

Chapter 16

Where There's A Will

THE PUBLIC ROOM in the police station had gone deadly quiet. Emma looked around to find everyone staring at her as if she'd suddenly lost her mind.

"Henry Collins is at Toorangabbie station," she repeated. "We need to fetch him."

Nathaniel was the first to find his voice. "Captain," he said, turning to Daniel. "Can I hire the *Mary B* for the day?"

"No," Daniel replied, earning a startled glance from Emma, "but I can take you to Toorangabbie and back if you pay for the wood." He winked at her, a gleam in his eye. She should have known better.

"Deal," Nathaniel told him. "When can we leave?"

"As soon as steam's up. You might need to lend a hand to keep the fire burning."

"Um, do you think you might need a policeman?" Emma put in. "Mr. Collins might not come back willingly, and the police will need to hear what he has to say in any case." If only it was what they needed to hear.

"You're right," Nathaniel said. "Constable? Can we arrange that?"

"I'll get the Sergeant, Mr. Pickles."

But Sergeant Donovan wasn't so easily convinced. As Emma listened to his arguments about wasting police time and resources, she suspected he didn't want to lose face by accepting that Henry Collins might have some relevance in the death of Old Mr. Pickles. He'd made it clear he had the culprit in his cells. She wondered how much her involvement had to do with his attitude, but whatever the problem, they weren't getting anywhere.

Constable Smith seemed to remember he'd left a visitor with their prisoner, and went to fetch Alex, who added his own voice to the argument once he knew what was at stake.

"He could have information about a murder," Alex argued, frustration evident. "What does a man have to do to get arrested?"

"Refuse to pay his bills?" Emma suggested. Alex looked at her. She nodded, and he grinned as understanding brightened his face.

"Sergeant," he said loudly and clearly, "I want Henry Collins arrested for non-payment of his account with my livery stable. The man's been living on credit everywhere for these past twelve months. I insist he be arrested immediately."

"A debtor is he? In that case," Sergeant Donovan said, "Constable, draw up the complaint and we'll go arrest the man. We know his whereabouts, and I believe transport is available. Is that correct?"

"That's correct, Sergeant," Nathaniel replied, and thumped Alex on the back.

With the paperwork taken care of, it was agreed that both the Sergeant and Constable Smith would join them on the *Mary B*. Emma was sure the policemen liked the idea of getting out of the office for a few hours, but it also might take the two of them to bring Henry Collins back if he proved difficult.

"Make sure you hear what Henry Collins has to say when the police talk to him, Mr. Pickles," Emma advised Nathaniel, as they made their way back to Watson Street. "And don't be afraid to ask some pertinent questions of your own."

"I intend to, don't you worry."

At home, she found Janey busy baking for tomorrow's picnic and asked her to make sandwiches for the men to take for lunch on their journey. "I'll help," she told her, as Janey looked as if she were being tasked with too much, "and I'll help later with getting everything ready for the picnic as well."

She would have preferred to go with the men on the *Mary B*, but she didn't want to get under Sergeant Donovan's feet. Henry Collins wasn't going to speak to her in any case. She figured she'd be more of a hindrance than a help. Half an hour later, she and

Janey waved the steamer off, with both Abe and Darcy on board.

After eating their own lunch, Emma and Janey spent the rest of the afternoon in the kitchen. There were cakes and bread to bake, and cordials and sandwich mixes to make. At least Emma had something to occupy her hands, if not her mind.

"Emma, you already done put bakin' soda in that cake mix," Janey said, as Emma stirred another teaspoonful into the dry ingredients for a sultana cake.

Emma stared into the bowl. "Did I?"

"You did. No, don't do that," Janey grabbed the bowl before Emma could dump the contents into the slops bucket, which was where a lot of her baking attempts ended up. "Give it here now. You peel them eggs for the sandwiches." Janey shook her head as Emma picked up a hard-boiled egg and cracked it down hard on the wooden bench. "It's okay. It's not wasted," Janey assured her. "I'll fix it."

"The only thing I care about fixing is having Janet come on our picnic tomorrow," Emma admitted, as she viciously cracked another egg.

Janey gave her a sideways glance. "It's not good, is it?" Emma shook her head. Janey didn't say anymore, wise enough to let her take out her concerns on the eggs.

It was almost six o'clock when the *Mary B* steamed gently into the bank below the house. Emma and Janey were sitting on the verandah, resting after their busy afternoon. Emma went down the bank and greeted Darcy with a hug as he ran down the boarding plank.

Next off was Constable Smith, followed by Henry Collins, who cut her as if she were invisible, but not before she saw he was sporting a black eye. He was followed off by the Sergeant, looking pleased, then a bewildered Evan Laughlan. Alex and Nathaniel, both decidedly downcast, were the last off.

Seeing them, Emma wanted to cry. "What did he have to say?" she asked, expecting the worst.

"He said Father was alive when he left him," Nathaniel replied. "Tired, as obstinate as always, but alive."

"Do you believe he was telling the truth?"

"It would appear so. Claims it was his creditors he was running from, and he couldn't get back fast enough once he realised he now owned the steamers outright. Laughlan had told him father had died. They were just waiting for a boat to call in on the way upriver."

And we provided him with a personal service at no charge, Emma thought wryly. With nothing in return.

"So, if he'd known your father was dead, he wouldn't have run, would he?" Nathaniel nodded. "Did he put up a fight? I notice he had a black eye." Though it had more colour than she would have expected if it had been inflicted in the past several hours.

Nathaniel gave what was almost a laugh for him. "That was Laughlan. Apparently, he'd put money into some investments Collins had told him about and lost everything."

"Collins even seemed happy to be spending a night in a jail cell for the charge I lodged against him," Alex put in glumly.

"Probably feels it's the safest place to be right now," Nathaniel said, staring into the distance. He took a shuddering breath, his voice now sounding as if wrenched from his heart. "They're taking Janet to Melbourne on Monday."

"We can't go on that picnic tomorrow, Daniel," Emma told him, when he and Abe had finished shutting down the *Mary B*. "We just can't. There must be something, something we can do."

She pushed aside the thought of all the food she and Janey had spent the afternoon putting together. Let it go to waste. The food was of no importance in the light of Janet's situation.

"Come sit down, love. Janey," he said to the girl, who was hovering, frown lines marking her normally smooth skin, her dark eyes troubled, "make us tea would you?"

The girl disappeared inside without a word, ushering Darcy and Abe before her, her silence a sign of the worry they were all under. Daniel guided Emma to the chairs on the verandah and they sat, but Emma was up again almost immediately, pacing, struggling to make sense of what she knew, and the odd bits that had been niggling at her mind just out of reach.

Old Mr. Pickles, surprising the family with the terms of his will. Samuel Rasmussen's refusal to speak to the police, or even to provide any real help for the family. Charity and Grace's acrimonious relationship. Grace's need for money. Everything, around and around in her head, a thread appearing now and then, and tantalisingly slipping away again. She walked up and down the verandah, as Daniel sat and watched and waited.

"I think I know how it happened, Daniel," she said eventually, although the threads she'd woven together felt tenuous, "but how do I prove it? There is no proof. I mean, anyone in the house could have done it, really. I think I know who did, and why, but…how do I get them to admit it?"

"Emma…"

"See, even Mr. Rasmussen believes Janet is guilty. And no one will gainsay Dr. MacArthur. He's the voice of authority where medical expertise is concerned."

"You mean he's wrong?" Daniel asked, unsure.

"He's not wrong in what he claims could have happened, but it's not the only way. He's not looking at all the variables. He likes a simple black and white answer I think." And certainly not to be challenged by the likes of her. None of them, Samuel Rasmussen,

Sergeant Donovan, would allow her to talk them down from what they believed.

"And none of them are looking at the people involved, and what's at stake for them. Nor how desperate they might be. Because whoever did this is desperate and frightened, and Janet isn't either of those things.

"Well, she's frightened now, of course, but...she'll be on her way to Melbourne on Monday, Daniel," she said, turning to look at him, solid and safe before her. Janet had that too, solid and safe in Alex, in her family. She didn't need to kill over an inheritance. "It'll be that much harder to fix it once they've taken her to Melbourne ..." She turned away and took another step.

"Wait." Daniel grabbed for her hand again before she resumed her pacing. "What do you need to do? What has to happen?"

HENRIETTA OPENED the door of the Pickles residence in answer to Emma's knock. It was just before eight in the evening. She'd left Daniel and Darcy at home, building a monster tower of blocks and reliving their journey to Toorangabbie.

"Is Sergeant Donovan here yet?" Emma asked.

"He is. But he didn't bring Janet."

No, he didn't believe he had it wrong, especially after hearing what Henry Collins had to say. It was up to her to change his mind about that. She just hoped she could. Henrietta led her to the dining room where the family were gathered around the table. They were all there. Nathaniel, Charity, Grace, Miriam, Jonathan, and Alex. The chair at the top was empty, waiting for Mr. Rasmussen.

It hadn't been easy, getting up the nerve to visit him at home, hoping he would be at home, and convincing him to hold the reading of the will tonight, before Janet was taken to Melbourne. Daniel had gone with her as moral support, and because he didn't want her walking around town on her own as the night drew in, but the end result of this would be up to her.

It didn't help her confidence that Mr. Rasmussen hadn't given any sign that what she suspected was correct, either. But at least he had listened and agreed to come.

Emma greeted everyone, and Jonathan stood and pulled out a chair for her. Henrietta took the seat on the other side of Emma.

"Is this your doing," Jonathon asked her, his voice low. She nodded. "Why didn't you let me know what was going on?"

"I'm sorry," she said. "It all happened rather quickly." She couldn't very well tell him she hadn't wanted him involved. Sergeant Donovan was looking pleased with himself, sure that he had the guilty party already in his cell. If he knew she had engineered this gathering he would no doubt be pleased to see it fail.

The clip, clop of hooves and swish of wheels reached them from the street. Henrietta went to the front door and a few minutes later ushered Mr. Rasmussen into the room. He was accompanied by his clerk, Mr. Thrum. Nathaniel found another chair for the clerk, who sat to the side, notebook open on his knee.

Introductions were made around the table, Mr. Rasmussen nodding amiably to Grace and Miriam, whom he hadn't met before. The anticipation in the room was thick and troubled as he removed papers from his briefcase. Spreading them out in front of him he began the preamble.

"We are gathered here to hear the reading of the last will and testament of Augustus Charles Oscar Pickles, dated the 15th day of March 1878..."

Nathaniel snorted. "The Ides of March. He did have a quirky sense of humour."

"That's one way of putting it," Charity commented grimly.

Mr. Rasmussen cleared his throat. "Being of sound mind, etc., etc., I leave the bulk of my estate comprising the house at 36 Connolly Street, Echuca, with its entire furnishings and fittings, and the contents of my personal deposit account at The Bank of Australasia, currently with a balance of some 1,500 pounds..."

"Janet is getting all that?" someone said.

Mr. Rasmussen raised his voice, "…to be shared equally between whoever of my three children, Charity Amelie Pickles, Nathaniel Oscar Pickles, and Grace Delia Hewitt nee Pickles, survive me. In the event that I outlive all three, the estate as described will be shared equally between my surviving grandchildren."

There was a moment's stunned silence around the table as Mr. Rasmussen paused for those present to take in what he had revealed.

Nathaniel laughed. "The old bugger," he said, and immediately clapped his hand over his mouth.

Tears were running down Grace's cheeks, of relief no doubt. Miriam swayed as if about to faint, and Charity sat with her mouth open.

"There are several smaller bequests," Mr. Rasmussen went on in his normal tone. "A hundred pounds each to both my granddaughters, Janet Naughton, nee Pickles, and Miriam Hewitt, should they not inherit the estate, fifty pounds to Henrietta Pickles, my favourite daughter-in-law…"

"His only daughter-in-law, the old fool," Henrietta said, wiping a tear from her eye.

"…and bequests of twenty pounds each to the Ladies Benevolent Society, and the Sailors' Welfare Fund." Mr. Rasmussen looked around at those seated. "I gather this dispersal was not what you were expecting. Most of you anyway." His gaze met Emma's.

"Our father told us he was leaving the house to my daughter, Janet," Nathaniel said. "I'm not sure why he would have said that."

"He did it because he was a contrary old man," Charity said, finding her voice at last.

"He was," Emma said quietly but clearly, "but he liked a peaceful, ordered life, and grown-up children who sniped at one another over the dinner table irritated him. Telling you he'd left the house to Janet seems to have been done to shock you."

"But he lied to us," Charity cried. "What did he hope to achieve by that?"

"Perhaps he hoped you'd behave better toward one another," Emma said, "but I very much doubt he would have wanted what came later. You see, what he told you that evening gave you all an agenda.

"You three, his children, wanted him to change his will in your favour, but when that opportunity died with him, the only way you could inherit was by preventing Janet from doing so. And one way to achieve that was to frame her for his murder. Which was plausible, because she had a motive to kill her grandfather before he could change his will and disinherit her, even if she claimed she didn't want the house."

"Of course she would want it," Grace said.

"Perhaps," Emma replied. "But the question remains. Did Janet kill her grandfather? Or did one of you frame her for causing his death?"

Chapter 17

Emma Forces the Issue

THE SILENCE that greeted Emma's words wasn't the same as that which had welcomed Mr. Rasmussen's announcement of the inheritance. This one was edged with outrage and horror.

"That's a disgusting claim, and totally without any merit or evidence," Charity spat. "No one in this family would indulge in such underhanded behaviour."

"But Janet has been charged with murder, Charity," Nathaniel reminded her.

"Murder is at least honest," Charity reasoned. "A blow struck in anger, when one's mind is troubled. But to do it to deliberately put the blame on someone else? No." Emma thought she had a point there. Had Charity ever wanted to kill someone? Her sister Grace perhaps? Or her deceitful lover?

"Do you know how it happened?" Jonathan asked.

"I believe so," Emma said."

"Well, as you are obviously trying to get Janet acquitted," Charity said, "that means you believe either myself, Grace or Nathaniel are the guilty ones. Which of us tried to frame her? Or are we in this together?"

"Well, the three of you did have a motive, Miss Pickles, as I explained, but you aren't the only ones. Are they, Miss Hewitt?" Emma said, turning to Miriam. "Your mother has received her inheritance. There is no further need for lies. Will you tell the truth now?"

"Me?" Miriam did a good job of looking astonished. "What are you talking about?"

"What indeed?" Jonathan echoed. "You need to explain."

Emma nodded, not taking her eyes off Miriam. "Your grandfather wasn't just sleeping, as you claimed, when you went into the parlour sometime before three o'clock on Wednesday, was he? You found him dead, and you were devastated. He wouldn't be able to change his will now. So, you came up with the idea of discrediting Janet, of getting her out of the way so the estate would go to his children after all."

Emma took a breath, and forced her fingers, linked together on the table, to remain relaxed. Everyone was staring at her as if transfixed. It was now or never.

"I believe you wrote the note first," Emma explained, "the one you claim your grandfather wrote asking Janet to come at once. Then you went for a quick walk to deliver it to the Tearoom. When you returned, you hit your dead grandfather on the head and left the firewood on the floor. You then stayed nearby, getting in the way in the kitchen while you waited for Janet to arrive.

"You needed to keep an eye on where everyone was so you could intercept anyone who tried to enter the parlour before she did. Janet had to be the one who went in and found your grandfather. You must have been delighted when you saw she'd picked up the firewood."

"That's not true," Miriam cried, her voice shrill. "He wasn't dead when I looked in on him. He was sleeping. I told you. My mother had spoken to Grandfather that morning and he said he was going to make it right. That's why he sent for Janet. And she killed him because he was going to change his will, and she wouldn't get the house. And I didn't go to the Tearoom to deliver a note."

"Thank you for that information, Miss Hewitt. But your grandfather didn't need to change his will, did he. Janet was never going to inherit. He was always planning on leaving his estate to his children."

"Yes, but Janet didn't know that, so she killed him before he could change it."

"Ah, but you didn't know it either, did you? You all believed Janet was to inherit, so when you went in to speak to your grandfather and found he had died, you came up with this plan to discredit her."

"No, I didn't. Jonathon, tell her I wouldn't do something like that."

"Mrs. Berry, I find these accusations more than a little unsettling."

"I'm sure you do, Mr. Inglis, but I don't believe it's going to be all that difficult to prove," Emma told him. "In fact, once I'd worked out what must have happened, I found there was more than enough evidence." There was a definite stirring of interest among the family at that.

Emma didn't add that the evidence was mostly circumstantial. She believed she could present a case, but there were also arguments that could be raised to explain away everything, and she was sure Jonathon would be able to come up with them all. She had to hope she could wear down Miriam.

"I'm very interested to hear it," Jonathan said now. Emma nodded.

"Henrietta, what time was it when Janet received the note asking her to come and see her grandfather?" she asked.

"It was a little before three," Henrietta replied, turning to Emma with hope in her eyes. "I was annoyed because it was about to get busy for afternoon tea. I wanted to know why my father-in-law couldn't have spoken to Janet while he was there for lunch, and what could be so important she had to go right away. Janet said he must have come to his senses and was going to change his will, so she was eager to go and see him."

"Did you see the note, Henrietta? Did you recognise it as something your father-in-law could have written?"

Henrietta seemed to struggle with her reply for a moment. "It was on a page torn from a notepad like the ones he normally used," she admitted. "The handwriting was shaky, barely readable but," she tipped her head to the side, "his hands had been shaky for some time."

"And do you remember what the note said?"

"It was very short. 'I need to speak to you. Come at once. Grandfather.' Something like that. I was surprised at how abrupt it was, not like him at all, but I thought if he was having trouble writing, I suppose it made sense that it was short."

"Either that, or the person who wrote it didn't know how he would normally express himself."

"Really, Mrs. Berry, is that the best argument you can come up with?" Jonathon challenged.

Nathaniel objected. "I can't think of any reason why my father wouldn't have said 'please.' That came as automatically to him as breathing. That note doesn't sound like something he would write."

Henrietta nodded. "And to make it sound urgent, and call Janet away at such a busy time. It wasn't urgent. For him at least," she said glancing at Miriam, who was staring straight ahead.

"It's an anomaly to keep in mind," Emma said, prepared to move on as it wasn't a point she could win outright, "but who delivered the note, Henrietta? Miss Hewitt claims she didn't."

"No. It was one of the young lads that are usually around the street."

"Did you recognise him?"

"Not really. He ran in, dropped it on the counter, and ran out again. I barely saw him, but it wouldn't be hard to find out who it was. You would just have to ask around."

"Something for the police to look into, perhaps," Emma said.

"If I find it necessary," Sergeant Donovan said.

"I had it delivered for Grandfather," Miriam said. "When I went out for a walk." Charity gave a snort, as if she doubted Miriam did anything for anyone but herself.

"You had the note delivered for him?" Emma asked. "And just when did he ask you to do that? You said he was asleep."

"He, he was. The note was lying there on the tea table."

"And you just took it on yourself to deliver it? So why didn't you? The Tearoom is only a block and a half up around the corner. You could have gone there yourself."

"I didn't feel like walking that far. We'd already been out walking a lot that day."

"No, that's not why. You sent the lad to deliver it because he could run, and you were in a hurry. You needed to get back to the house. You didn't want anyone finding your grandfather dead before Janet arrived, isn't that right?"

"No, no, it wasn't like that. I was just trying to help."

"Do you remember what the note said, Miss Hewitt? 'I need to speak to you. Come at once. Grandfather.' Why would he write a note with an urgent summons such as that, and then just leave it lying about. It makes more sense that your grandfather would have rung for Peggy to deliver the note as soon as he'd written it. If he was the one who had written it."

"This is still just your interpretation of the facts, Mrs. Berry," Jonathon said. "It doesn't prove anything."

"No, it doesn't, does it? It's all just an interpretation of the facts. Just like Dr. MacArthur claiming the blow to the head caused the heart attack, despite there being no blood at the wound because his heart wasn't pumping because he was already dead. He was, wasn't he Miss Hewitt?"

The girl was beginning to shake. Emma took a deep breath and changed her tone.

"But then in the parlour the note disappears," she said, as if puzzled. "Janet put it on the tea table but amid all the accusations and confusion, it disappears.

Tossed into the fireplace in case its authenticity should ever be questioned. Janet had no reason to get rid of it. Quite the opposite in fact. She needed it to prove she had been summoned, that she had a reason for being there.

"In the same way, the firewood gets removed from the basket and kicked under Mr. Pickles' armchair. A useful piece of physical evidence, despite there being no proof as to who had used it to hit the old man on the head. It just added confirmation as to what had happened. Janet would have been more likely to have thrown it in the fireplace, as Sergeant Donovan accused her of doing, if she'd been guilty of using it."

Emma paused for a moment. "All very neat, but it leaves us with a great deal of reasonable doubt, and two possible suspects. The circumstances can point to either Janet – or to Miriam."

"No," Grace cried, half rising from her seat.

Mr. Rasmussen cleared his throat. "That is a succinct summation, and certainly a reasonable one, based on what is known."

Jonathon had tensed beside her.

"Miriam," Emma appealed softly, leaning forward, "it's time to tell the truth. This wasn't murder. You aren't going to be charged with killing your grandfather. You found him dead, didn't you? Sometime in the afternoon, after Henry Collins left the house, your grandfather suffered a fatal heart attack."

The girl was shaking now, tears running unchecked down her face.

"Miriam, can you spend the rest of your life knowing you sent your cousin Janet to the gallows based on a lie you told? Can you live with that?"

"Miriam?" Jonathan almost whispered.

"We had nothing," she choked out. "Father left us with nothing. I was afraid. You would've had to take care of my mother. I was afraid you would change your mind and not wish to marry me when you learned we wouldn't inherit anything from Grandfather."

There were gasps of surprise and dismay. Emma sat back and closed her eyes for a moment. She hadn't enjoyed what she'd done, but at least Miriam wouldn't face the fate that had awaited Janet.

Grace, her face as white as the handkerchief clutched in her hand, stood and moved behind Miriam's chair, leaning down to put her arms awkwardly around her daughter's shoulders.

"It's all right. We can start again. Somewhere we're not known. Adelaide, or Perth perhaps. Yes, Perth would be best, it's furthest away. We have the money now. We'll be all right. We'll get through this."

Sergeant Donovan cleared his throat. "It's not that simple, ma'am. Interfering with the body of a deceased person is a crime. Miss Hewitt, I'm arresting you on the charge of defacing the corpse of Mr. Pickles Snr. You need to come with me."

He at least had the decency this time not to produce handcuffs. Grace walked out ahead of him with Miriam, her arms tight around her daughter whose head rested on her shoulder. As he left the room, the Sergeant glanced at Emma and gave an almost imperceptible nod. Was that approval, or a 'watch it, lady' warning? She really must remember to ask Daniel about him.

At the sound of the front door closing behind them the room erupted with tears, hugs and cries of joy. Even Charity seemed pleased with the result, but Emma did wonder if part of it was because she felt Grace had gotten some payback.

Henrietta, Nathaniel, and Alex left for the police station with Mr. Rasmussen, who promised to have Janet released immediately. As he went by, Nathaniel patted Jonathon on the shoulder.

Henrietta raised her eyebrows in a question to Emma, but she shook her head and stayed where she was. She needed to speak to Jonathon, who hadn't moved since Miriam had confessed.

"I am so sorry it turned out the way it has, Mr. Inglis," she told him now.

"So am I, Mrs. Berry." When he didn't say anything more, Emma said goodnight to him, and to Charity, and walked out of the house.

"There you are." Daniel got up from a seat on the verandah.

"We came to walk you home, Mummy," Darcy said. "You have to see the tower we built. It's much, much, much bigger than Jemmy's."

"I'll enjoy seeing that."

"I saw Nat," Daniel said, putting his arm around her shoulder as they walked off down the street, Darcy hanging onto her hand. "Everything worked out well, he said. All because of you. Well done."

Emma felt exceedingly tired. "As well as could be expected, anyway," she said, thinking of Jonathon.

Epilogue

A Sunday Picnic

IT WAS A CHEERFUL boat load of passengers that steamed away upriver the following morning. They were all seated on the front deck of the *Mary B*, the best place on a day like this, the sun almost overhead, a soft breeze in their faces. Their joy at the pleasant, sunny day and prospect of a picnic, with no murder hanging over them, was tempered by the thought of Miriam Hewitt's future.

Nathaniel reported that Mr. Rasmussen had offered to represent her at trial. "He says it won't go to Melbourne. It can be dealt with here. She'll get the best defence on offer, anyway," he said, tilting back his chair, and stretching his legs.

Emma was pleased to hear that and wondered if Mr. Rasmussen had made the offer to compensate for his lack of help for Janet, believing, as he must have done, that the police had it right when they charged her. Miriam might even get off without any real prison time, but Emma wasn't overly hopeful about that. Women weren't supposed to be violent, and they were treated more harshly than men when they were.

"And Jonathan?" she asked.

"Devastated about Miriam, naturally," Nathaniel replied. "He moved himself to the Exchange Hotel this morning. I'm not sure he knows what he wants right now."

"He did tell me the other day that he was considering his future, even before this happened." Emma hoped whatever Jonathan Inglis decided would make him happy. He was a pleasant young man, and probably not as cut-throat as some barristers she'd read about.

"When it comes to his career, it will be a case of whether he wants to be a big fish in a small pond, or a small fish in a big pond," Henrietta said.

"Small fish, big pond," Janet said dreamily, her eyes closed.

Emma wondered if she was thinking of the seaside. Sitting a little further off was the nanny, Winnie, nursing little Katy who had fallen asleep. Emma was glad Janet had brought Winnie with them, so she and Alex could relax.

Janey had taken to Winnie, too. Perhaps she could teach the girl to be a little firmer with Colin, though she suspected it was Janet herself who spoiled the boy.

Right now, young Colin was shadowing Darcy and Jemmy, who were fascinated by the engine room where Abe was in charge, with Alex as his offsider. Abe was turning into a good practical engineer. If she hadn't lost Janey to the Tearoom, she might be in danger of losing Abe to the river. She hoped not. She could make use of him at home if there was a local demand for the herbal remedies she made.

She must remember to make up more of the echinacea lozenges. She'd told the man in the doctor's waiting room to call this week. And there was still that batch of liniment to make for the farmers, up-river.

"Have you decided yet about joining the Benevolent Society, Emma?" Henrietta asked, breaking in on her thoughts.

"I suppose I could," Emma said. At least she hadn't embarrassed herself in front of Mr. Rasmussen, so hopefully he hadn't said anything unflattering about her to his wife and daughter, which meant membership of the Society could be an option. And murder was the last thing to fear in that rarified atmosphere.

The bell rang from the cockpit signalling to the engine room to slow, and the *Mary B* nosed toward the bank where a patch of green and shade, and a little sandy beach, waited. It was the perfect picnic spot. As the *Mary B* came to a gentle stop, Emma stood and went to help Janey unload the food hampers.

* * *

Next in Series

Death of a Lady

Emma's herbal remedies are growing in popularity as town folk take advantage of her expertise. Until one of her customers is found dead in their bed. Sergeant Donovan is keeping his options open this time. For now. But when the coroner finds the dead woman was poisoned, rumours spread like wildfire. Was the poison in Emma's concoction? Emma sets Janey to chat up the dead woman's servants, while she investigates her life for a possible motive. But when another death brings matters to crisis point, Emma's friends urge caution. Retreat or risk becoming the next victim. Either way she's in trouble. *Death of a Lady* is due out in early 2026.

About the Author

Irene Sauman writes historical cozy mysteries. Under her pen name, Rennae Todd, she writes cozy mysteries in a present-day setting.

Irene is a retired historian who grew up on a vineyard and orange orchard by the Murray River in New South Wales. She was an avid reader and started writing stories when she was nine years old (including some really dreadful poetry).

Now living in Western Australia, she has three children and four grandchildren, and a sister who beta reads her books for plot holes and to see how quickly she can solve the mystery.

When not writing (or reading), Irene watches tennis, plays croquet, and has a reasonably green thumb, which means very little dies in her garden, unlike in her cozy mysteries.

Irene and Rennae share a website where you can learn more about their books, which are available in digital and print.

https://irenesaumanauthor.com

Follow us on Bookbub to be notified of a new release.

https://www.bookbub.com/authors/irene-sauman

https://www.bookbub.com/authors/rennae-todd